MÁRIO DE SÁ-CARNEIRO:
The Ambiguity of a Suicide

Giuseppe Cafiero
Translated by Peter Christie

London | New York

Published by Clink Street Publishing 2017

First edition.

ISBN: 978-1-911525-57-8 paperback,
ISBN: 978-1-911525-58-5 ebook

To Paola, Melissa and Emiliano

HENDERSON & CRASTON
Detective Agency
21 Osnaburgh St., Regent's Park
London, England

to Mr David Mondine
Piazza della Borsa, 8
Trieste (Austria)
30 June 1916

Dear Mr Mondine,

I had thought that you were lost in a boundless sea. They reported to me that perhaps you had rashly embarked on a very poor looking and rather treacherous ship. Thus difficult in keeping a rough and hostile sea at bay. A true ship, or your improvident propensity to embark? It seemed to many, including those fortunate enough to know you, that you wandered with your mind in horizons that seemed to open up to bizarre and ambiguous investigative adventures.

Were you dreaming perhaps of enterprising journeys without precluding any destination? Perhaps the determination to flee was the most evident sign of a fantasy that foretold satisfying paradigms. Undoubtedly mental doodles, which must be relied upon in the ambiguity of human will.

I was not intending to rummage among dirty clothes. Mine was only the mute aspiration of a miscreant drunkard. And the imagination will certainly have had some regrettable responsibility. I never believed that you had rashly yielded to improbable fantasies of opportunity and necessity. Perhaps urges of melancholy financial needs?

I thought it plausible, for example, that you might have been carried away by stories in taverns amidst chronic drunkenness there in Istria. One glass leads to another. Slivovitz or something else? Mellow flavour and white transparency. Also the fragrance. Wild plums, and alcohol up to 70%. An old and rash habit of the peoples of the Balkans. For us it is malt: the sacred malt, also whisky sometimes with endless toasts in honour of King George V. In exclusive clubs, certainly not in harbour taverns. At the Caledonian, or the Colonial Club, or also the Thatched House, or even the Wellington. Right in the heart of London while you had the faculty to go wandering as an unaware drunk regurgitating bile of past slaveries and fantasising about your next assignment.

Yours was always a job well done since you had the merit and the diligent ability to undertake even hateful and ungrateful exercises in order to satisfy desired wishes and strict provisions that we entrusted to you.

To follow, with absolute professional skill, even as far as engaging in a deceptive and supportive friendship – that James Joyce, a Dublin writer, who, having abandoned Trieste, went to Rome to settle accounts with the Holy Roman Church. It was 1906, do you remember? Now, in the year of grace 1916, have you reconciled yourself?

In these ten years, sometimes heinous duties and often unbearable events have overwhelmed me and have marked my country, often harmed our peoples, inexorably disconcerted our minds. Personally, I have passed these years and still spend my existence in a placid indifference, continuing to investigate in order to offer, in tacit exclusiveness, diligent services to the Secret Service Bureau from my office in Osnaburgh Street.

As far as I know, there have been unfortunate events where you are, and it is for this reason, I believe, that you had, so they tell me, the determination to no longer take to the sea and to take refuge in the silence of discreet work which did not involve others.

Thus you wisely avoided an unjust war, also because you live not far from the Stabilimento Tecnico Triestino and the San Marco dockyard which saw the launches of the battleship Viribus Unitis, *steel with nickel chrome armour and with 12 Škoda guns of 305 mm/45 calibre and 12 of 150 mm/45 calibre, 18 guns of 70 mm, two machine guns of 47 mm and four torpedo tubes of 533 mm, the battleship* Radetzky *with two vertical triple expansion engines, 12 Yarrow boilers, two propellers and a power of 20,000 HP, 38 Škoda guns of various calibres, and the armoured cruiser* Sankt Georg *with 20 guns of various sizes and barrels of 40 or 45 calibre, and two River Mk 2 torpedo tubes of 450 mm. Horrible war machines.*

This is information provided to me by the Secret Service Bureau.

Hence I was very reassured to have found you unharmed and in need of remunerative work.

So, we come to the present and the reason why I am writing to you. I have the urgent need for you to return for some time, albeit for a short period, to your past activities as investigator. At the moment, I require your valuable assistance, which will be, as is my practice, well rewarded. I will now recount the why and the how.

I have received a desperate request to provide aid and support to Fernando António Nogueira Pessoa, a little-known writer of Portuguese nationality, who has had the misfortune to lose in Paris, some months ago (in April to be exact, I am told), in an unfortunate accident and in unclear circumstances, his dear friend who went by the name of Mário de Sá-Carneiro, a poet, playwright and writer and son of Commander Carlos Augusto de Sá-Carneiro, currently director of the port and the railways of Lourenço Marques in Mozambique.

It is necessary to investigate this unfortunate occurrence in order to appease the disconsolate soul of this Pessoa, who is a man afflicted with manic disturbances of ambiguous depersonalisation. Thus he avoided and avoids giving vent to his sadness, but in his soul, to hear some of his most intimate friends and acquaintances who seem to live in a rather fictional world, he yearns to know the truth about the death of Mário de Sá-Carneiro.

Not to obtain definite information about the circumstances and conditions in which that unfortunate incident occurred, but to know that a thorough investigation was carried out, and if it arrived at an incontrovertible truth.

Pessoa is a man of such passionate and muddled sensibility who – in a madness managed in a very personal way by contentedly experiencing, I am told (something which in truth I do not at all believe), the proliferation of his personality – is happy to live in an ambiguous incoherence and in an indeterminacy of reality. This sees him as a participant of multiple personalities without, again I am told, being aware of his fits of unreasonableness.

Do you think this is possible?

According to unfortunate gossip to which it is inappropriate to listen, he has even invented friends born from his intimate thoughts, soul companions with their own singular personalities. Of this I will provide you further details later, certainly to confute such slanderous rumours and to give you a more appropriate account.

This Pessoa is also affirming that "Não é o tédio a doença do aborrecimento de nada ter que fazer, mas a doença maior de se sentir que não vale a pena fazer nada[1]". *Thus, or so I am told, he is often overcome by a frantic desire to be confined in a sanatorium, because he perceives that he is about to fall prey to a raging psychasthenia. Thus neurasthenia subjugates hysteria so that he manages to dominate very well any outburst; hence his hysteria tends to be frenetic and delirious. Moreover, he feels, often and without first having evident symptoms, a certain and indecipherable apathy, as well as the sensation of a bipolar disorder. This syndrome takes hold of his life and he is forced to share it – at least that is what I have been told although its significance is difficult to comprehend – with people or characters outside of his 'ego', in other words with alter-egos that have their own existence and lead a life that is intertwined, subtly and in a disturbing manner, with his.*

Perhaps you will understand better than me these dark tendencies, which are not explained in a clear and understandable manner in any medical textbook that I have consulted.

It also seems that this Pessoa loves to exhibit, through these adventurous and indecipherable friends, different types of knowledge – philosophical and syntactical – which are very useful to his equilibrium.

On my part, I have nothing further to add, neither comments nor particular appeals, concerning what I have written thus far.

The ambiguity of the facts, which some persons have been good enough to narrate to me and which concern Mário de Sá-Carneiro, appears to me marked by destabilising specificities in a mish-mash of truth and unreliability, of health and madness, of very determined wills and disordering abulias, of mental confusions and disturbing rationalities.

---

1 Fernando Pessoa, *The Book of Disquiet: "Tedium is not the malaise of boredom from having nothing to do, but a more serious malaise: feeling that there is nothing worth doing".*

At this point you will ask how I received this awkward information and the invitation to investigate the incident that led to the death of Mário de Sá-Carneiro in Paris.

My old and kindly acquaintance, Dr Abílio Fernandes Quaresma[2]*, who delights in investigations and anything else involving the solution of indecipherable enigmas and very complex puzzles, even mathematical and chess-related ones, wrote to me inviting me to take the job as he is currently unable to do so – dedicated as he is – since he is confined in his apartment on the third floor of Rua dos Fanqueiros among smoky Peraltas cigars and alcoholic disorientations, carefully studying, in a complex and orgiastic sequela, the infinite series of problematical chess moves proposed by that talented player who responds to the name of Akiba Rubinstein during his thrilling encounter with Gersz Rotlewi.*

Above all, Dr Quaresma was reluctant to personally take on the task since the emotional closeness that binds him, in an anomalous and unselfish manner, to the poet Pessoa does not allow him to be calm and disinterested, as he would have to be, in dealing with this incident.

In truth, I hold very little belief in such banal justifications. Instead I am convinced of Dr Quaresma's congenital lethargy in having to abandon, in order to probe complex links and to encounter friends and acquaintances of Pessoa who at times appear unreal and thus likely to recount incongruous truths, the rituals and habits that make his life acceptable in its sensuous rationality with regard, for example, to his immoderate drinking and smoking without any disturbance.

Nevertheless, he said that he was willing to accompany the investigator, thus you if you accept the job, if you, for reasons concerning the investigation, were to go to Paris. Yet he would certainly not be interested in visiting the place where Mário de Sá-Carneiro died and in meeting those who were close to him in the days before the unfortunate incident, maintaining this with unusual stubbornness. He would willingly accompany you provided that he had, when he wished, the opportunity to spend his days accommodated at a table of a reputable

2 Some scholars (cf. Marmion Bur, *Characters, Heteronymy and Mental Distress*, Stratford 1935) have stated that Dr Abílio Fernandes Quaresma is the protagonist of the detective stories written by Fernando Pessoa.

bistro. Indeed, he seemed to me very willing to meet with you after each of your explorations and after you have collected the statements of witnesses.

Thus there would be, I seemed to understand, the possibility of discusings the ongoing investigations, to help and suggest what to do. Indeed, I believe that Dr Quaresma is very interested in being involved in the investigation into the death of Sá-Carneiro when that investigation is carried out beyond the Portuguese border and especially in France where the alcoholic spirits are very commendable – although I hope that this does not mean absinthe or Fée Verte – and the cigars are excellent: La Aurora, Navarrenx or General Cigar.

I had the honour of being contacted by Dr Quaresma after he had first asked Arthur Conan Doyle to undertake the investigation, entrusting it to the sage and unparalleled expertise of Sherlock Holmes. However, Mr Holmes was about to make a permanent move, after so many exhausting investigations, to the countryside near Eastbourne in East Sussex on the southern coast of England, where he wished to spend his days devoted exclusively to philosophy and beekeeping. Mr Holmes also declined the invitation because of his innate reluctance to provide his services outside of his homeland. He violated this rigid prerogative only when he had to put an end to that 'final problem', which had led him to the Reichenbach Falls near Meiringen in Switzerland, in the violent conflict with his archenemy Professor Moriarty.

Mr Conan Doyle then suggested my name to Dr Abílio Quaresma as a very reliable investigator and a person who has in his employ only conscientious and competent people. Hence I thought of you, having already experienced your skill and your authority in investigative matters, albeit some years ago as I have mentioned. It would be essential for me that you deal with this case, of which below I provide further information that may be useful to you.

It is clear that you will have to investigate on the spot, that is in Paris, where the incident that deprived Mário de Sá-Carneiro of his life took place. Yet first you must go to Portugal to hear stories and take notes on what will be reported to you by three close friends of Fernando Pessoa. It was also, and appropriately, reported by Dr Quaresma that these three intellectuals are also kinds of alter-egos of Fernando Pessoa, that is men ineluctably involved in Pessoa's life in a very subtle manner, having an effect on what I earlier called his psychasthenia and bipolar disorder which often, but not always, involves a kind of deliberate simulation.

Simulation of what? In truth, I do not know how to answer that, if not believing it plausible based only on strictly intellectual motivations. If you can, find out from friends or read books on the topic so that you will best be able to deal with the situation.

The gentlemen in question respond to the names of: Álvaro *de Campos, Dr Ricardo Reis and António Mora*[3]*. Separately I will provide you with their addresses or at least where it might be possible to find them.*

The three gentlemen in question have lives burdened by very personal torments or ambiguous fixations that make them very particular, I would say unusual, people. They share the same poetic spirit, so I am told, since all three owe very much to the distinguished poet Alberto Caeiro da Silva who advised them to versify freely and in a very simple language. I inform you that Alberto Caeiro died last year of tuberculosis at a young age, only 26 years old.

I would like to point out to you, merely as a simple fact and nothing else, that Caeiro da Silva died at the same age at which our Mário de Sá-Carneiro met his death. Moreover, Álvaro de Campos, Dr Ricardo Reis and António Mora, as I have opportunely been informed, are followers of neo-paganism. I am sure that you, as a careful reader of philosophical subjects and an extremely cultured person, have knowledge of this orientation. However, to offer you a different and very personal interpretation, I would like to recall that the Portuguese neo-paganism involves derivation from Greek primitiveness, since it considers the Christian religion a product of the decay of the Roman world. Criticism as non-compliance with the equilibrium that determines civilisation, but also as a degeneration of ideas and sentiments. I could say, in short, that it embraces Epicureanism.

---

3 Some scholars (cf. Marmion Bur, *Characters, Heteronymy and Mental Distress*, Stratford 1935) have stated that Álvaro de Campos, Dr Ricardo Reis and António Mora are merely heteronyms of Fernando Pessoa.

It is necessary, therefore, that you act in the best of ways. Frequenting Álvaro de Campos, Dr Ricardo Reis and António Mora without any prejudice so as to glean from them accurate information about Sá-Carneiro. I would like to inform you above all that while Álvaro de Campos is pagan mainly for rebellion, Dr Ricardo Reis is so for appearance and António Mora for intelligence. Thus I was told.

I offer you some other specific information about the three gentlemen, clarifying however that the information is fragmentary and often without evidence. Accept it then with a certain benefit, but bear in mind that it is possible that, in the ambiguity of the collected information, there may be something truthful or that what seems apparently true is merely the result of ambiguous gossip.

Álvaro de Campos, for example, is subject to a lethargic temperament, to a tireless inertia that leads him to suffer insidious nervous crises. He does not have a real job even though he is a naval engineer. Hence he lives thanks to a decent annuity from a wealthy family. He travels to unusual and distant places, including the Far East, and he visited Britain for a certain time. He has disgraceful propensities to self-destruction and to the senseless desire to return to live in a now-legendary world.

Dr Ricardo Reis, educated in a Jesuit college, is a highly appreciated physician. A convinced monarchist, he wishes to leave Portugal to travel overseas, perhaps to Brazil. He is a Latinist of high calibre thanks to the teachings received and is Hellenistic by culture. A poet of excellent quality, he loves to subject his poetic vein to extreme discipline so much so that his verses are marked by a profound musicality, containing harmonic and bucolic chords.

António Mora was the first author to have written exhaustively on paganism and neo-paganism, stating, among other things, that the purpose of art is to totally imitate nature, thus rejecting any uncertainty and limitation of sentiments. Afflicted with paranoia and hysteria he is confined to a sanatorium. It seems that his 'delirium' has as its reference point Christianity which, in his opinion, has disturbed his life, creating in him a propensity to onanism, that is to castration in the development of ideas.

I have reported to you what I am able to report about these three personages. Now I would like to point out that the travel expenses and any others that you might encounter during your investigation, even unexpectedly exorbitant ones, will be completely undertaken by me.

Your compensation will be, as usual, solid and substantial, and it will be you yourself to determine it.

I look forward to hearing from you, certain that you will not disappoint an old friend and one of your unconventional employers.

With best regards,

Angus Craston

p.s. I am sending to you, in an accompanying envelope, reports, pamphlets and publications on Fernando Pessoa and Mário de Sá-Carneiro. I am convinced that you will know how to put the material to good use.

II

Lisbon. *Lisboa antigua. Lisboa, velha cidade, / Cheia de encanto e beleza*[4]!

A harbour. Enchantments.

The odours nourished an ambiguous imagination. A nose for ancient waters. The sense of smell, then. Remembering a childhood in Trieste. Sea and salt air. Duino was then in his heart. A manor house corroded by time. White, skeletal, dried by the sun. Progenitor of imperial deaths. The ocean is another thing. Gusts of an Atlantic wind. Gazing at conquered lands. Lisbon.

A silent, melancholy morning. Looking around. Anxiously yielding to disquiet. Worn embankments breaking up soft backwashes. Beyond them a boundless ocean. The harbour was a certain refuge. Solitude and past songs.

"Juncada de rosmaninho / Se o meu amor vier cedinho / Eu beijo as pedras do chão / Que ele pisar no caminho.[5]*"*

The voice of Maria Severa Onofriana[6]? The lady of the '*fado*'. She knew how to play the guitar magnificently. Strings parallel to the sound box. To then abandon life at the age of 26. Tuberculosis is a killer. "*O gosto que tinha o Fado, / Tudo com ela acabou.*[7]" Rest in peace Maria Severa Onofriana, there in the

---

4 Ancient Lisbon, Lisbon, old city / *full of charm and beauty.*

5 *"Strewn with rosemary / If my love comes very early / I kiss the stones on the ground / He stepped on while walking".*

6 Maria Severa Onofriana (1820 – 1846), known as *A Severa*, is considered the first singer of '*fado*' (destiny), attaining incomparable fame after her death at only 26 years of age.

7 *"The flavour that the fado had / All disappeared along with her".*

cemetery of Alto de São João. Lisbon. Her voice is still lost in pregnant melancholies.

Memories drawn from a *Baedeker.* LEIPZIG, 1912. Cm. 16 x 11.5, pp. LVI, 508. Bound in full red cloth. Being flogged by nostalgic flavours that belonged only to time. Perhaps to a past. Forgetting. Rhythmic steps and now finding an unusual and pretentious magazine purchased from a shabby newsagent.

Orpheu 2.

Abril-Maio-Junho, 1915. *Revista trimestal de Literatura.* Propriedade de: *Orpheu,* L.[de]. Editor: António Ferro. Endereço: Luís de Montalvor al 17 de Comibho de Forno do Tijolo Lisboa. Tipografia: Tipografia de Comércio. 10, Rua da Oliveira Carmo – Telefono 2724. Lisboa.

Good printing, excellent paper, with the singular collaboration of the Futurist painter Santa-Rita Pintor. A pseudonym. Guilherme de Santa Rita was his real name. Eccentric with his *"sensibilità mechanica, sensibilità lithographica, sensibilità radiographica, interseccionismo plastico"*. The texts then. Here is the list of authors. Fernando Pessoa, Mário de Sá-Carneiro, Ângelo de Lime, Luís de Montalvor.

A quick glance.

Fingers hungrily flipping through the pages. Pages tousled by the wind. Pausing from time to time. Recalling Pessoa. *"E a sombra duma nau mais antiga que o porto que passa / Entre o meu sonho do porto e o meu ver esta paisagem / E chega ao pé de mim, e entra por mim dentro / E passa para o outro lado da minha alma...*[8]*"*

It seemed then that one could be enriched by controversial knowledge. Moving beyond any physicality. Perfidiously dissolving any psychic distress. Pungent cerebral sensitivity. Pessoa, in fact. Seductive emotions. The unconscious distracted. Gazing in mirrors that reflected imprecise images.

Only for Pessoa or also for some of his singular friends?

---

8 Fernando Pessoa. *Oblique Rain: "...And the shadow of a ship older than the harbour passes / Between my dream of the harbour and my view of this landscape / And it arrives at my feet and enters within me / And it passes to the other side of my soul."*

New, symbolic and intuitive forms of knowledge. Thus intertwining memories, paradigms and erudite readings in a cruelly ambiguous manner. Also, pleasant and unpleasant mishmashes. Yielding to regrets and consolations. Half-closing one's eyes. Wandering with the mind. Mnemonic journeys? Better to dwell on the annotations. Better than many foolish pastimes and naive distractions. Meanwhile the waters of the harbour seemed motionless.

Behind now, the Bugio Lighthouse. Imposing sentry at the entrance to the estuary.

The Tejo, the river, appeared ever more alluring. A place of eternal and melancholy loneliness. The river gracefully widened and narrowed, providing appropriate landing spots. Briefly a flat stretch greeted a steep hill marked by a jumble of old buildings. Terracotta rooftops. The '*lioz*' limestone gave luminosity to the buildings with its gradations. From grey to yellowish to pink.

The pier, meanwhile, was wide and burdened with confused noises. Also with a dense, uninterrupted chatter. Galician inflections marked by time. Also several British ships at anchor which certainly noted the names of the German ships being resupplied. Suddenly the commotion of carts pulled by yoked mules. Doca da Alfândega, in fact, where the steamships of the Societé Torlades arriving from Bordeaux were docked. Then the gloomy customs building. Nearby in a vast basin were boats of some *Companhia de Pescarias*, crowded together displaying hulls and towering masts. Here and there several *muleta* with their large sail, or several *Barco Rabelo* with a square sail, or a *sotovento* with slender silhouette. Among the many boats, also the double sails of some dories.

The sky was a sly light blue in the haze of a sweltering day. Filamentous cirrus clouds were knotted on high without however providing any shelter from the blinding light of a full scorching sun. Every so often the reflections wounded the eyes scanning the surroundings. A hand occasionally acted as a dauntless visor so that one's vision did not suffer accidental injuries.

Not far away were rails set in a double row on which rattled some '*carro electrico a dois troleys*' that threw out sparks in clusters almost as if they were shooting stars. Rarely there passed a few silent horse-drawn *'americanos'*. The people, meanwhile, were quick to chase either the *'carro'* or the *'americano'*, always uncertain where to await them. For 30 réis one could travel through the entire city.

On one side, shoeshine boys were busy at their craft, quartered along a facade of low buildings amidst footrest boxes equipped with an arsenal of brushes and polishes of all types and colours. Also crippled beggars eagerly asking for some réis while displaying deformities due to injuries suffered in rash jobs or to war wounds. Then sellers of precarious junk. Crowded benches along roads suffering under a torrid heat. Even dirty *capilé* vendors anxious to extend, for one real, that refreshing blend of barley coffee, sugar, lemon and cool water.

Was this the people that had practised and still practised a bold and brazen piracy? Were these the ravenous filibusters of the seas scattered well beyond the horizon?

This is what was recounted by those fearing the Lusitanians. Books also informed that the piratical voyages of the Portuguese were deemed necessary to satisfy ambitions of conquest and trade. Targeted piracies. Also organised violence. Spices and slave trade. The Portuguese, in fact. And Pessoa and his friends?

History often taught that knowledge could be biased. Remembrances suspended in memory. Distant seas, it's true. Who remembered? *Cidade do Nome de Deus, de Macau, Não há outra mais Leal*[9].

Macau overlooking the China Sea. It was also reflected in the branch of the Si Kiang river. Thus began a terrifying colonial adventure. Pope Nicholas V was its singular apostle since he advocated the perpetual slavery of the indigenous peoples. *Dum Diversas* was the Papal Bull of 16 June 1452 that accompanied the *Divino amore communiti* of King Afonso V of Portugal. Assigning without delay all human and inhuman rights.

9 *City in the Name of God, Macao, no other is more loyal.*

"With the apostolic authority of this edict, we grant you the full and free power to capture and subjugate the Saracens and pagans, as well as other infidels and enemies of Christ, whoever they are and wherever they dwell; to take all types of assets, movable or immovable, which are in possession of these same Saracens, pagans, infidels and enemies of Christ ..." Incontestable words.

Hence they began to organise military expeditions against the Muslims. To prepare a *placet* in reducing the natives to perpetual captivity. Otherwise it was appropriate to convert them, turn them into docile Catholics. Or into domesticated servants. *Placet, placet* as the Bible invited with ineluctable words: *"Servants, be subject to your masters with all fear; not only to the good and gentle, but also to the forward.*[10]*"*

Nisi conversi fueritis et efficiamini sicut parvuli, non intrabitis in regnum caelorum[11].

It happened first at *Gôa Dourada*[12], on the Arabian Sea. The Jesuits did what, it was supposed, it was legitimate and necessary to do. Forced evangelisation became an ineluctable necessity and a mission became a place of religious government for the explorations. A viceroy then left a mark on that land facing the sea. To control maritime traffic. To administer the dominions. From the Persian Gulf to India and the Far East. The evangelisers thus became apostles of excellent efficiency.

Regrets?

Much more convenient to control the routes of commerce and the commerce itself. Spices and slaves.

Ever since Vasco da Gama. Commendable intuition to bring a Jesuit with him. Adequate subjugations provided edifying examples. A good excuse. Defeat the infidels. He who loved a spice so much, pepper for example, had a valid excuse to engage in wars of conquest. Thus trade became a profitable art. Naval force. From East Africa to the Indian Ocean. From the Atlantic Ocean

---

10 Bible, 1 Peter 2, 18.

11 Bible, Matthew 18, 3: "Except ye be converted, and become as little children, ye shall not enter into the kingdom of heaven."

12 Golden Goa.

to West Africa. Not at all discontent, with sordid justification, to be accompanied by Jesuit missionaries because they were auspices of holy missions.

Distinguishable signs of absolute powers. It then became a mandatory requirement, as it was possible to read in any history of voyages beyond the Pillars of Hercules. Was it then necessary to update the *Baedeker*? A controversial choice if one recalled the writings of Giovanni Battista Ramusio[13].

Voyage to India on behalf of Giovanni da Empoli.

Giovanni wrote: *"I believe without a doubt that, with God's help, not only will the most serene King of Portugal acquire great honour and wealth, but I also dare to say that, in the space of 50 years, there will be converted many people, whom God will grant his infinite grace."*

Brutal conquests, no doubt.

Thus the mind pursued tales of massacres and extorted riches. It is good to look around. To forget past readings?

The sea, then. Also, a shoreline. Undertows. Placid waves lapping into themselves.

The Tejo River came down from Fuente de Garcia. However, they were other waters that died meekly in a vast delta. The men who governed did not know the pleasure of those waters. Private business. Obscure cabals. Portugal. Meanwhile, Bernardino Luís Machado Guimarães the Republican decided the fate of the country. It was rumoured that he was a wealthy merchant, necessarily noble. Conquered wealth. And if they were only ambiguous rumours?

The coast was sandy and punctuated here and there by natural cliffs. David Mondine observed it with surprising wonder.

Meanwhile, one could read in the newspapers that the government had begun to recruit an expeditionary force. With reluctance, certainly! Europe was at war. Do not antagonise those who should not be antagonised. Obligatory choice. Imposed perhaps?

---

13 Veneziano was the author of *Delle navigationi et viaggi*, published between 1550 and 1606.

Siding with the Triple Entente[14]. Thus sending two infantry divisions and one infantry battalion on bicycles and one of sappers. In total about 55,000 men. Western Front. Directing them into the *Corpo Expedicionário Português.* Also, nine artillery batteries with guns and howitzers of 75, 105 and 155 mm. Only ten cargo ships. No warship. Better not to frequent the seas, thus avoiding a clash with the German Kaiserliche Marine, with the Austro-Hungarian k.u.k. Kriegsmarine and with the Ottoman Osmanlı Donanması.

A bizarre appearance of the sea, observed David Mondine.

Meanwhile, his memory tried to recall some distant ocean. Readings. Remembering the occasion when he saw the reports by Amerigo Vespucci, Vicente Yáñez Pinzón and Pedro Alvares Cabral or the letters by Martim Afonso de Sousa. Wretched shores where slave ships would have docked. Remembering what he had read. Remembering Angola when the king N'Gola reigned over the Mbundu.

In fact, the Atlantic had encouraged the landings. The ocean thus became a safe route to deport men. It was not enough to take ivory, rubber, spices from those lands. Human trade was more profitable. To repopulate the Americas. The Atlantic was not always benevolent. There were even tragic deaths. Storms and battered ships. Shipwrecks duly taken into account. The lifeboats were reserved for white men. Slaves in chains, fed with some frugal bowls of beans, corn and potatoes. The water ration was half a pint a day. Encouraging natural selection. From the market to the sales counter. Slaves at auction. Good business because the trade was profitable and sumptuous. Slavery soon became a sought-after practice. *Pombeiros* e *fumantes*[15] obtained substantial benefits.

A piece of paper was drawn from the hefty envelope received from Mr Angus Craston. Thus David Mondine had the

14 The Triple Entente was a political–military alliance of England, France and Russia.

15 Procurers and traders of slaves.

opportunity to read some eccentric verses that this Mário de Sá-Carneiro had composed. Perhaps in 1914.

"Eu não sou eu nem sou o outro / Sou qualquer coisa de intermédio: / Pilar de ponte de tédio / Que-vai de mim pasra o Outro.[16]*"*

Something must have been weighing on Mário Sá-Carneiro's mind. A prelude or an amen?

Travelling along the treacherous roads of life. A sign of immoral restlessness. Dying civilly or uncivilly after having rolled the dice that had marked loves and hates, tenacity and indecision, rebellion and surrender.

Also facing other possible unfortunate meditations. Seeking refuge in a dreamlike unawareness. David Mondine began to scrutinise the sea. Stolen memories in an agitated unconsciousness. Becoming lost. A unique beauty: so it seemed. The chatter subjugated the wishes of the glances. Interpreting the murmuring with the wise annotations of a *Baedeker.* Also, irritating interjections. Thinking about something else. Unpleasant memories of the conquests in Africa. And Fernando Pessoa?

Certain news. Why had he lived in Durban? A British colony. Natal. Sugarcane plantations, so it seemed. Blacks and Indians. The English had a strong preference for the Indians. The gulf that opened in front of Durban led straight to India. Forced colonisation. Then war between whites. Gold and diamonds were very appealing. No one held the salaried slaves of the plantations in high esteem.

Did Fernando feel shame and impropriety?

Perhaps he had something else to think about. Aspiring not to the probable but to the incredible. Adolescence seemed to be the time of thoughtlessness. Not even the sea could be a safe haven. Ships docked and departed laden with mineral treasures and wealthy men. Someone came to terms with his anxieties when he had the feeling of being able to converse with an alter-ego. An unpleasant story.

---

16 Mário de Sá-Carneiro, Indicios de Ouro, 7. *"I am neither I nor the other / I am something in between / Pillar of a tedious bridge / That goes from me to the Other."*

Although burdened with dark thoughts, David Mondine thought it appropriate to analyse as best possible the task assigned to him, even though he was troubled by a listless insecurity.

Gusts of wind.

Rethinking the events of which he had become aware. Neurasthenic disorders and unusual behaviours. Undoubtedly lettered men. Poetic ones, rather. Arrogantly revolutionary poets? Poets afflicted by neurotic lives. Relying on their mysterious unconsciousnesses? And what about their sluggardly manias? Or their restless wandering? Or the claustrophobic solitudes? Analysing profiles and declared ailments.

Consulting valuable and partially exhaustive booklets. Appropriate needs. Precious remnants recovered from a bookseller's shop.

Sammlung kleiner Schriften zur Neurosenlehre[17] and *Bruchstuck einer Hysterie-Analyse*[18]. Sigmund Freud!

Having read, annotated, transcribed. Remembering, in fact. Doctrinal but undoubtedly intricate readings. Fragments. Pedantic presuppositions. Understanding if possible meanings could or could not be merely contemplative dogmas. Phrases underlined so as to be recalled if necessary. Studies corroborated by evidence. Cases. Innumerable cases. An adequate sample? It seemed so. Who was without sin?

Primus lapidem mittere[19].

Biblical precepts. To influence those who were easily influenced? A tough life for someone investigating hysterical ailments. Being content with what he had in hand. Comparing what he knew or wanted to know by exploring books. Then? Reading with unusual fervour. Jargon. Ambiguity of words and accents. Seizing possible and impossible meanings. Also, fascinating readings. Indeed. *Bruchstück einer Hysterie-Analyse.* Volume in quarto. Lovely binding. Blue covers. Page after page. Browsing carefully.

---

17 *Collection of writings on the theory of neuroses.*

18 *Fragment of an analysis of hysteria.*

19 *Let him first cast a stone.*

Suddenly David Mondine realised that he had been touched by a kind of grace. Perhaps a true revelation. Guarantees? Certainly supports. Reconstructing the lives of the gentleman poets ... Sly statements of Professor Sigmund Freud. Hysteria, in fact! Was it? Didactically it could have been ...

Investigating and giving attention to the documents sent by Mr Craston, as appendices to the letter.

A first note, written in pencil, marked a clean sheet. *"De morbis mulierum."* Better to avoid old affirmations. Clear! The Hippocratic school should have been considered outdated. Sigmund spoke of something else. Knowledge of the facts?

David Mondine read and evaluated carefully.

No more therapeutic vapours or carbohydrate and mucilaginous amalgam or genital compressions to stem a hysterical compulsion. Something else. Or so it seemed. Even for men. Probably misogynists. Look inward and be able to say: *"Quem não se enoja de ter mãe por ter sido tão vulvar na sua origem?*[20]*"*

Is it so? Knowing one's own history.

Angus Craston had transcribed pertinent and observant notes. Remembering Fernando António Nogueira Pessoa. Pondering on what had been written as necessary and enlightening readings. Herr Freud! Hysterical stigmata. An indelible mark. It was what had to be in extreme circumstances. Therefore, what was written in the Holy Bible could have no value: *"From henceforth let no man trouble me: for I bear in my body the marks of the Lord Jesus.*[21]*"*

To think about it, those of Pessoa seemed to be merely human stigmata. There was nothing left but to carefully evaluate childhood events to understand an infancy that might perhaps parallel that of Mário Sá-Carneiro.

Was it since childhood that Pessoa had the tendency *"de criar personalidades novas, novos tipos de fingir que compreendo o mundo,*

---

20 Fernando Pessoa, The Book of Disquiet, 11, 5, 1913. *"Who cannot feel disgust for having had a mother, for having had such a vulval origin?"*

21 Bible, Galatians 6, 17.

ou, antes, de fingir que se pode compreendê-lo[22]"? And Captain Thibault, Chevalier de Pas[23] and others he had forgotten? Perhaps to flee from a reality that depressed him. Going, as an orphan, to an unfamiliar country after losing his father Joaquin de Seabra.

Instead Mário had lost his mother. Then he walked the path of bourgeois prosperity. And the philosophical vision of the life of Mário de Sá-Carneiro? Selling and underselling his life. Familial objects.

The mother, Maria Madalena Pinheiro Nogueira, Pessoa's mother, had been a courageous woman. Mourning was mourning. And mourning oppressed like a sad mantra. Difficult to escape. Also Jorge, Fernando's younger brother, had surrendered to death. A tragic and prophetic mantra. Looking around and observing with disquietude the alienating episodes that seemed to mark a family.

Donna Dionísia Estrela Pessoa, paternal grandmother, lived her life amidst equivocal and rash imbalances, exhibiting obscene chattering and uncontrollable aggression. Also a pathological aversion to children, marked by overpowering and violent rages. Hence the asylum seemed to be a necessary place in which to give her appropriate attention. From that a hereditary madness?

It was worrying thinking about that. Someone even feared it for his entire life. Madness lurking in the shadows?

He could certainly not forget. Also hallucinations, since an unreasonable madness seemed to dominate the family. What? Fearing for himself. And there was something else. Only uncontrolled disorders? Someone also spoke of rash personalities, multiple personalities.

The friends? Fernando's close friends were Álvaro de Campos, Ricardo Reis and António Mora. A maze of assumptions without having in mind whatever was being talked about. Illusions. Rewarding a juvenile solitude. Dreams could often betray.

---

22 Letter from Pessoa to Adolfo Casais Monteiro (director of the magazine *Presença di Coimbra*) of 20 January 1935: *"to create new characters, new types of pretending to understand the world, or better pretending that one can understand".*

23 Pessoa used the first heteronym when he was only six years old.

Therefore it was necessary that David Mondine conduct an investigation dictated primarily by the will to explore following the documents that Mr Angus Craston had sent. Herr Freud, meanwhile, lavished careful exegeses.

One paragraph seemed significant even though the note might have appeared unclear, perhaps cryptic. It was nevertheless very intriguing.

David Mondine lingered curiously over it. Also an incentive for a careful examination.

"A very fertile ground on which is implanted a pathogenic memory", was written somewhere.

For Senhor Pessoa?

The death of the father or the madness of the grandmother?

Meanwhile Pessoa had moved to Durban, in English Natal, when the mother had remarried. Thus becoming a stepson. Was it possible then the onset of an unfortunate hysteria caused by a lost father and another one acquired?

Travelling across the Indian Ocean. Very different from the Atlantic Ocean. Those waters did not experience tumultuous and terrifying tropical storms. It was necessary, meanwhile, to submit to the strict British customs and traditions. English Natal. True or false Puritanism? And the onset of a stable hysteria? It was what it was.

Also a time of insatiable reading.

So many good choices.

But there was an exceptional and engaging book: *The Pickwick Papers* of Dickens, because, as Fernando wrote: *"Mr Pickwick belongs to the sacred figures of the world's history. Do not, please, claim that he has never existed: the same thing happens to most of the world's sacred figures, and they have been living presences for a vast number of consoled wretches. So, if a mystic can claim a personal acquaintance and clear vision of the Christ, a human man can claim personal acquaintance and a clear vision of Mr Pickwick."*

Recovering his inspired ambiguities through the pages of a book. Not at all a moment of ephemeral evasion.

Rebelling against an oppressive and grey reality. Finding

himself in a world that the imagination seemed to render unique. Leaving aside rules consumed by habit and by a rigid upbringing. Also strict social rules. Everything had to be very 'British'. Thus subtle humour and false morality were necessary acquisitions for social cohabitation. Exalting himself with disbelief and metaphorical representations. Wanting therefore to be something that he was not?

Mr Pickwick was alive far beyond the pages of a book. Did he begin to imagine another or others? Also Alexander Search[24] who had written *A Very Original Dinner.* 1907. Or Charles Robert Anon[24] with his five philosophical meditations and his poems. They were other himselves. Difficult to find his way in that mish-mash.

Mirrors could have been of some help. Meditating on mental premises. Something was inevitably changing. Perhaps it had already changed. It would certainly change even more rapidly with the years.

24 Heteronyms of Pessoa when he was living in Durban.

III

Mr Craston had sent very precise, albeit disorganised, notes. Many indications on how to undertake that unwieldy investigative task. Firstly, exchanging impressions on the life of Mário de Sá-Carneiro with some of Fernando Pessoa's supposed friends. Hence it was necessary to identify with whom it was possible to trade ideas. Then to determine with what pretexts and verbal schemes necessary to ask specific questions about the life that Mário had led in Lisbon. It was also appropriate to obtain some information about the alleged suicide, in Paris, of that young man who had died at just 26 years of age.

Mário de Sá-Carneiro was a poet quite unknown to most people, remarked one of Mr Craston's notes. To some instead he was known as a person with odd propensities to theatricalisation.

However, the physical features were certain. Information received from those who knew him or thought they knew him well. All carefully transcribed by Mr Craston. Large, clumsy and shy. Like a stout sphinx. A part that divided his hair almost in two. His torso enclosed in a double-breasted coat that seemed to strangle him while he moved uncertainly about the streets of Lisbon with a lost, painful look, marked by tedious regrets.

The friendship that bound Mário to Fernando Pessoa was indisputable. A very extravagant friend since it was rumoured that he had had the courage to write the verses: "*Perdi-me dentro de mim / Porque eu era labirinto, / E hoje, quando me sinto, / É com saudades de mim.*[25]"

---

25 Mário de Sá-Carneiro, *Dispersão*, 1914: *"I am lost within myself / because I was a labyrinth, / and now, when I feel myself, / it's like losing myself."*

Never take for granted what belonged only to hearsay. And if that were true, it was not certain that it might be a sign of principal attention. Imagination and ambiguity often deceived. Rumours and truths might or might not have been the face of the same coin. And thus friendships. In truth, only devious gossip seemed to have something to say about this. Or specular games. Multiple specular games. Other lives, in short. Lives that belonged and did not belong to those who offered themselves so ambiguously in telling stories. And on and on using their talents for not at all original propositions.

Wounds from resolute and determined resentments. Weird anomalies. Also moody statements.

Sed Vulgo Dixit. Amen.

Mr Craston had also advised great caution.

The only certainty was that ineluctable confirmation had come from the Hôtel de Nice in Paris that Mário de Sá-Carneiro, born in Lisbon on 19 May 1890, and who was staying in that hotel, had really died, by presumed suicide, on 26 April 1916. A certain José Baptiste d'Araújo, a Portuguese shady dealer, and a police commissioner had certified his death. The funeral was held on the 29th. A simple fir coffin, "*covered with a black cloth with silver fringes*[26]" was accompanied on a modest hearse to the Pantin cemetery, just beyond Boulevard Sérurie outside the Alemagne gate, by a small procession of friends. Perhaps just three.

Hence jotting down information became a necessary, almost indispensable, task for David Mondine. As well as the evaluation of reams of notes, chaotic and hastily transcribed. Mr Craston had sent many of them to him as an undoubted support.

Learned and explanatory paragraphs. Succinct and disordered biographies. Hasty transcriptions by employees inattentive in drafting letters. Notes that had often lost any trace of chronology. It had happened then that David Mondine came upon, in the bedlam of papers, the note, certainly penned with the

26 From the writings of Xavier de Carvalho.

unsteady hand and indecipherable handwriting of Mr Craston, that mentioned Dionísia, Fernando Pessoa's grandmother, confined in the Rilhafoles asylum, there in the hospital buildings of Campo dos Martires da Patria. A very intriguing circumstance, Mr Craston had written without providing any explanation. In the margin a note in which was underlined: *"the fear had then become, so it seemed, panic."*

No other explanatory note.

Perhaps that the friendships formed had become intimate only with those who had some sort of congenital madness harboured in their blood? That Mr Craston meant something about the reason for that close friendship between Mário and Fernando? It seemed that someone feared that the madness might contaminate him. At the very least Fernando Pessoa, it appeared. However, it was wise not to judge intimate and unknown paranoias without knowing their underlying causes. Someone should have reminded Pessoa, with unfortunate and constant insistence, to bear in mind that primary familial infirmity.

Therefore, it was difficult for him to make his way amidst enmities and survive with impunity well knowing that someone, often and at his discretion, might mention that something pettily farcical and mad could accompany him throughout his entire life. It was almost necessary then to be involved in friendships with people who could well understand that fear without uttering offensive words or bringing up hereditary defects present in his ancestry.

He began, abruptly and unexpectedly, to hear *"um bom dia e boa noite*[27]*"*, without knowing who had said it. He looked around and found himself to be alone. Perhaps reflected images that had suddenly been animated? Yet he could not understand what had happened when he made sure that he was alone and that there was nothing around him that could reflect an image. He continued on, becoming the protagonist of that verbal pronouncement that seemed directed toward himself. Not thinking though.

---

27 *"a good morning and good night".*

Not imagining that it was not humanly possible that he was no longer himself. It was necessary then to meet the others who, it seemed almost a fact, had taken possession of him. A bad situation. Attempting perhaps desperate measures. He then began to look at himself in a mirror. Something happened since there appeared in the mirror a face that was not his own. Yet a face that he knew well. Another face. The face of a self that was no longer himself. Grandmother Dionísia undoubtedly had had a hand in this.

Thus avoiding the annoyance of having to provide further details. Keeping close those friends who were not bewildered by his distressing neurasthenias because there persisted other anxieties, various worries, frustrating ills of the mind. Mário de Sá-Carneiro, for example.

Mário had entered Fernando's life through an open door in 1912. Then in 1913, 3 February, with a letter. A copy of that letter was enclosed in a leaflet sent by Mr Craston. Explicit and clarificatory. *"O que é preciso, meu querido Fernando, è reunir, concluir os seus versos e publicá-los não perdendo energias em longos artigos de crítica nem tão-pouco escrevendo fragmentos admiráveis mas nunca terminadas. É preciso que se conheça a poeta Fernando Pessoa, o artista Fernando Pessoa... por lúcido e brilhante que ele seja.*[28]*"*

An occasion that solidified a brotherly friendship. Thus Pessoa became *meu amigo de alma*[29].

Poetry was often able to conceal affections and madnesses, but also flattering accolades and undoubted needs of brotherhood. Fernando was a poet of oblique verses, of saying without being able to say everything, of the aristocracy of versification, of syllabic games so that his spiritual reality would have the upper hand over the mediocrity of a petty literature. And from a young age. Especially in English.

---

28 Letter from Mário de Sá-Carneiro to Fernando Pessoa of 3 February 1913: *"What you need, my dear Fernando, is to finish your poems and publish them, without wasting energy in long critical articles or even in admirable but never completed fragments. It is necessary to know the poet Fernando Pessoa, the artist Fernando Pessoa ... lucid and brilliant as he is".*

29 *My soul mate.*

Were the asylum horrors vigil companions of altered lives? Around a corner, grandmother Dionísia could watch, suggest paths, teach how to avoid pitfalls. Having a *"rebellious nature that raised up against any constraint*[30]*"* when he was composing poems and lyrics in different languages.

Lisbon was engaging. It was not easy to live there.

Upon his return from Durban, Fernando was welcomed to Lapa, recalled Mr Craston in a note. Lapa was the neighbourhood where his maternal aunts, Rita and Maria Xavier, and his grandmother Dionísia lived. In Rua da Bela Vista 17, to be precise. Fernando then wrote almost a confession: *"Know'st thou what madness is? / Wonder not. All is mysteries. / Ask not. For who can reply?*[31]*"* Misanthropy soon convinced him to seek refuge in alcohol and tobacco. Degenerate escape routes. Not being able to do anything else. This he knew well. Saving himself beyond any written word since many words and many writings had become prerogatives of other selves. The non-selves, that is, that were born from the self with rash ease. Just like their stories.

Degenerations. Moral perversions. Saving himself somehow. And the incurable nature of the symptoms?

Grandma Dionísia was undoubtedly a very uncomfortable presence. Madness lurking in the wings. Who really existed? Disconcerting ambivalences. To exit from the magic circle of madness or remain there and manage a tragic existence in his own way? Find a solution for the abyss of the mind by playing with masks of his being. Changing appearances. Crediting himself with disparate and ambiguous professions. Expressing opposing political orientations. Being himself without having to be so on account of profound needs. Grandma Dionísia was a very uncomfortable presence.

Confessing right, left and centre his psychic disturbances. Real or only imaginary? Deceiving even the friends to whom he

30 Sigmund Freud, *Studies on Hysteria.*

31 Fernando Pessoa, *Flashes of Madness IV*, 2, 18-20.

was bound. Thus living an ambiguous life, feeling perpetually alien in whatever place, and preserving the dignity of tedium.

The solitary life that became a normal practice. Mr Craston recounted that Fernando had inherited from Grandma Dionísia a small patrimony and a silent and hidden madness. 1907. Going on his own. Going free for ... Other streets, other homes.

Intimate needs. Perennial peregrinations. This is what made Fernando, according to Mr Craston's account.

Then taking up residence in Rua da Glória. Then in Largo do Carmo 18. Followed by Rua de Passos Manuel 24. Then moving to Rua Pascoal de Melo 119. Finally, in Rua D. Estefânia 127, to live with his close and specular friends. Himself and the other himselves. Without the monotony of having to constantly deal with a real himself.

The mirror was a silent and disturbing presence.

Mr Craston had been explicit in his sibylline accounts by means of barely scribbled memoranda. Only precise clarifying notes. Many, in truth. A morass of names and persons. Enigmatic logs for a mentality that had been raised in the British spirit. Not at all humorous. Mr Craston was, in fact, devoid of humour. Fernando had then returned to Lisbon. Hence Mediterranean peculiarities. Orthonyms and heteronyms. Surprising and reckless losses. Who was who? Mr Craston's messages were explicit. Emphasising the appropriateness of not being deceived by malicious gossip and cruel mystifying desires. Never being outraged listening to rumours marked as impudent and imprudent.

Indeed, restlessness could generate envy since Fernando was stating, as a stubborn and rash citizen of the imagination, that "*A superioridade não se mascara de palhaço; é de renúncia e de silêncio que se veste*[32]".

Persons or characters?

None of all that apparently. Understanding explicit needs. Finding himself in the need to ... Or in no need? It seemed only

32 Fernando Pessoa, 21 November 1915. Scattered notes: "*Superiority does not wear a clown's face, but dresses itself with sacrifice and silence.*"

a fictional world in which he could exist beyond preconceived schemes and visions coded by a single person.

Being and wanting to be someone else in order to probe reality in a different manner so that he could have for himself a different life story, a different profession and a different existence.

A complex mental game.

Meanwhile, Mr Craston had been very clear: do not try to understand what was not permitted to be understood, but interpret, albeit without understanding, what was needed to be interpreted. At least for the investigation. Set up meetings without worrying about the ambiguously existential nature of the interlocutors: whether they were *'existing'* or *'created to exist fantastically'*. Fantastically?, David Mondine had asked reading the memorandum. Regrettable and inappropriate adverb, he had suddenly thought.

Mr Craston had also noticed his unfortunate clarification, so much so that he had promptly rectified that expression in a subsequent memorandum sent by cable. Not *'fantastically'* he had written, but *'appropriately'*, or rather *'in a suitable manner'*. Referring to certain precarious identities, it should be understood.

David Mondine shuddered thinking about the complications that prefigured the definitions of identities. Being forced to imagine identities without identity. Hence drawing forth from memory plausible meditative notions able to provide clarifying signs. David Mondine then asked: if *non-identity* meant lack of identity, what meaning was it necessary to give to identity so that one could support the existence of non-identity? Perhaps it was what was called heteronym?

David Mondine remembered that the envelope that Mr Craston had sent to him and that accompanied the letter of commission and clarification included a bundle of memoranda tied with a band bearing the words *"IDENTITIES or SIMILARS – items from philosophical learnings"* which was intended for Mondine's thorough or unthorough investigations of *'identity'*.

Thus Mr Craston must have ascertained – so David Mondine assumed – the appropriateness of sorting out and clarifying in some way the very obscure and volatile world of Fernando Pessoa.

The paper seal was quickly and breathlessly torn open. Thus David Mondine found in his hands a bulky mass of crumpled sheets of paper with sentences, sayings, syllogisms, statements, utterances and implorations highlighting what philosophical minds had expressed concerning the inscrutable lemma *'identity'.*

No chronological order had been given to those memoranda, just a simple and careless arrangement certainly dictated by memory in its cognitive frailty, so much so that it often allowed some memories to emerge according to sly and inexplicable rules. They were thoughts expressed by illustrious philosophers of the past.

He found himself facing a mass of reflections drawn from long past studies or he found himself examining transcripts prepared hastily by copying this or that thought certainly from a splendid encyclopaedia.

David Mondine thought of the *Encyclopædia Britannica,* or *A Dictionary of Arts and Sciences, compiled upon a new plan,* or *The Sum of Human Knowledge,* of which Mr Craston, as a scheming, curious and arrogant bibliophile, certainly possessed the latest edition. Presumably that of 1913, that is. Twenty-nine volumes. 28,150 pages. 44,000,000 words. Opaque Indian paper. Publisher: Cambridge University Press.

David Mondine began to browse through that bundle of memoranda with tenacious curiosity. With an apprehensive intent. To capture agitated thoughts and obtain standards and rules that would have facilitated in some way his knowledge of the mental tangles that perhaps plagued Fernando Pessoa. Were they really unwieldy obstacles?

In truth, they seemed merely an inexplicable maze of different personalities arising from a single mind, ready to become lost in realities pondered and suitably constructed so that those other personalities would have a way to exist. Something else? It even came to mind that, if he was in a world at the limit of a psychic squabble, he could hide in the identities of other people.

Indeed, it was almost appropriate to unconsciously create other personalities.

David Mondine then began to read fragments drawn from more profound philosophical enunciations. Almost synopses. Details that were comprehensible, almost as if he was a profound student of philosophical interests. He began with reasonings by Thales of Miletus which indicated his own thoughts on *'identity'* in a slyly intriguing manner. According to him, one could think of the totality of things only if one had the intelligence to observe them and to identify a set of unequals, that is of different things. Thus identity, which was inherent in the bold complexity of the multiple, managed to include in itself precisely those different things that were intrinsically part of that whole. A proposition which, although it may have appeared forced to those who did not understand it, was instead natural and could not escape someone who was curious about the uniqueness of unequals.

There was then transcribed, in a brief memorandum, the thoughts on the identities of different things by Parmenides of Elea. A game of subtle discernments, since he was claiming that everything existed solely on the basis of diversities. Anyone, by wishing it, could continuously change any premise because, at the same time, it was and was not. Very subtle satisfaction and appreciation since conjectural premises of any other kind were not foreseen. Being and not being at the same time. Thus avoiding the ambiguities of uncertainties.

David Mondine then began to reflect, with disconcerting uncertainty, about what was reported of the thinking of Anaximander. Taking for granted that the origin of all things was indefinite, or rather infinite. The identity of the different thing, as a constituent part of the indefinite, could be, in turn, only indefinite. Hence the whole and the different thing were, in their essence, only a unique, almost coinciding, moment. No ambiguity of interpretation or of verification was possible. Therefore, single and participatory acceptance, actualised in an inclusive infinite.

Mondine lingered for a few moments over Plotinus of Lycopolis, the recognised heir of Plato. Concrete and determined premises. Absolute verification. The unity of different things was essential and necessary for there to be existence. A *unicum* arising from many, from different things, from multiples. Therefore, it was inevitable and indispensable to convey the diversities in that *unicum* in order to arrive at a unitary essence. From simple and different principles arriving finally and resolutely at the multiple-unique.

Finally, Mondine considered Heraclitus of Ephesus, the pre-Socratic. Real multiplicities and the *unicum*. Proven facts and no errors of thought. A becoming that took into consideration the variations of one's being. Necessary evolution because the flux was able to metabolise the changes of considerations and oblique thoughts. All things were *'one'*, and *'the one'*. A view that resulted, in some way and inevitably, in a paradox since, as the same Heraclitus stated, *"The road uphill and the road downhill are one and the same"*.

David Mondine then began to scrutinise the notes sent by Mr Craston. He read and pondered without well understanding what those philosophical details were meant to clarify, as they were so ambiguous in thought and expression. They had done nothing but trigger a subtle interplay of muddles where everything seemed to appear different from any learned enunciation without ever refuting what was quite different from that same enunciation.

Knowing and not knowing, then! Indeed knowledge involved a fictitious indoctrination, specifically an end in itself, while not knowing implied the acquisition of wills that perhaps were able to give meaning to intuition and to an original desire for knowledge.

Dejected, David Mondine put the memoranda in his pocket.

He had little faith in his ability to distinguish concepts so philosophically different and confused. However, he had the merit of ignoring the help that Mr Craston seemed to want to offer him, mainly because he had doubts about the care and truthfulness with which Mr Craston had transcribed hints, prefixes and confused concepts concerning those philosophers. David

Mondine believed it appropriate merely to imagine the unstable consciousness that had animated Fernando Pessoa.

Ambiguous people or deliberately ambiguous characters born from the ambiguous impertinence of an ambiguous man who had nothing sensibly healthy about him if not the same ambiguity and the desire to lose himself in the proliferation of ambiguous identities.

Perhaps a puppeteer who had learned to be a puppeteer without realising that he was one. Unconsciously, then, he began to bring to life the puppets that he himself had created so that in some way he could enliven their existence.

Thus the management of the parts was tiring. Discovering also that "*leitura é uma forma servil de sonhar.*[33]" Correct to affirm then that "*Se tenho de sonhar, porque não sonhar os meus próprios sonhos*"? To extricate himself from himself? A complicated affair for someone who did not understand that infinite game that some loved to play with themselves. The rest had to be as if he decided to create circumstances, ways and expressions that involved another existence that had in itself the existential curriculum of an own ambiguous and principal existence.

Being deceived and deceiving.

Theatrical representation. Wearing a mask with impunity and becoming a character that the mask envisaged and thus imposed. Then changing the mask and drawing forth another existential reality. Perhaps it was more appropriate to let others wear the masks. A game? An ambiguously heterodox life.

Meanwhile, someone had filled his days as a correspondent in foreign languages. Fernando António Nogueira Pessoa, in fact. Information from Mr Craston. Import and export companies. An aristocratic profession. Financially rewarding. And without regret he had declined the chair of English Literature offered to him by the chancellor of the University of Coimbra. Dr Coelho de Carvalho had been his promoter. An absolute must to avoid

---

33 Fernando Pessoa, Scattered notes. *"Literature is a servile way to dream."*
"If I must dream why not dream my own dreams."

the derisions of a certain Álvaro de Campos, who would have mocked him because he, Fernando António Nogueira Pessoa, represented a certain poetic and *saudosista* philosophy and could not in any way be a professor. There was nothing left but to wander the streets of Lisbon frequenting welcoming and salutary locales.

Cafés especially, frequenting A Brasileira in Rua Garrett 12, Martinho da Arcada in Largo D. João da Câmara, Cafè Montanha in Gaveto de rua da Assumpeão and Abel Pereira da Ponseca in Rua dos Fanqueiros[34]. Places of drinking and salubrious inebriations.

Becoming lost in the city, trudging about sadly inebriated after leaving the cafés. The mind seemingly clear. The resistance to alcohol robust. Unperturbed, despite having consumed large amounts of spirits and wine. Healthy mixtures. An exciting life in the evening, often looking at a full glass. Did he never think about possible cirrhosis of the liver? The glass was especially comforting. Going about Lisbon with impeccable aplomb. Extreme care in his appearance. White shirt. Bow tie perfectly in tone. Impeccable dark grisaille suit. The eyeglasses gave a detached dignity. A chevron moustache. Homburg hat in soft felt. In winter his coat seemed to be sliding off him at any moment. A caressing wind often bent back the collar of his paletot. The firm *Lourenço & Santos* which was an impeccable outfitter? Much more *O Eduardo Martin & C.* or of *Armazen de Moda* in Rua Santa Maria? Absolute respectability.

Also, lost loves. He remembered well, without wishing to recall which loves.

Memories that never, he thought, should have become real memories. Downing then another invigorating glass. Possibly acquiring an effervescent inebriation.

A quick look in a broken and dirty mirror. Recognising the shadows of an alcoholic euphoria. Reciting from memory or inventing there and then? *"Com mão mortal elevo à mortal boca /*

34 Lisbon cafés frequented by Pessoa.

Em frágil taça o passageiro vinho, / Baços os olhos feitos / Para deixar de ver[35]*"*.

Losing himself without abandoning *saudade.*

A far off voice intoned a melancholic song. *"Recordações do calor / E das saudades, o gosto / Que eu vou procurar esquecer / Numas ginginhas.*[36]*"*

Abrasive itineraries.

Smoking assiduously. The obscure pleasure of puffing so that his emotional life had full satisfaction. Evading his intimate sufferings. Wilfully. The cigarette and I. Rendering ineffective any introspection. Smoke. A strand of smoke. Madama Butterfly? *"Um belo dia, vamos perceber. Um fio de fumaça proveniente do mar.*[37]*"* Thus losing himself in a desired infirmity. Savouring *"No cigarro a libertação de todos os pensamentos. / Sigo o fumo como uma rota própria, / E gozo, num momento sensitivo e competente, / A libertação de todas as especulações / E a consciência de que a metafísica é uma consequência de estar mal disposto.*[38]*"* Charutos & Cigarros.

Walking quickly to reach the *Tabacaria Costa,* or the *Tabacaria Polar,* or the *Tabacaria Rocha,* or the *Tabacaria do Campo de Santa Clara.*

Then, taking into account what Mr Cranston had written in one of the memoranda sent in the envelope, David Mondine began to feel strange disquietudes that seemed to become obsessions. *Geração de* Orpheu[39]. A myth, the myth. Not looking back.

---

35 Fernando Pessoa, Selected poems: *"With mortal hand I raise to mortal mouth / In a fragile cup the light wine, / Cloudy are my eyes / In order not to see".*
36 *"Remembrances of heat / And of melancholy, a taste / That I shall seek to forget / In some ginjinhas."*
37 *"Un bel dì, vedremo levarsi un fil di fumo dall'estremo confin del mare" (One fine day, we'll see a strand of smoke arising over the horizon of the sea).*
38 Álvaro de Campos, The Tobacco Shop: *"In the cigarette freedom from all thoughts / I follow the smoke as if it's my own path, / And I enjoy, in a sensitive and fitting moment, / Freedom from all speculation / And awareness that metaphysics is a consequence of feeling ill."*
39 A group of people who sought to introduce Modernism to Portuguese arts and literature by means of the quarterly magazine *Orpheu.* The group included the poets Fernando Pessoa, Mário de Sá-Carneiro and Almada Negreiros, and the painters Amadeo de Souza-Cardoso and Guilherme de Santa-Rita.

A Portugal regenerated. Modernism? The magazine *Orpheu* had ceased publication at the third number. Facing rash perceptions.

Moving toward other fields of knowledge.

Clarifying with himself or forgetting himself in imperative necessities? Esotericism, automatic writing, mysterious narratives. Also heretical views. It was in this way that he sought to rein imaginary friends into reality. By revealing himself or by waiting for them to reveal themselves. Fatal turmoils. Meanwhile, a friend had found death in Paris.

O Senhor Fernando Pessoa.

Recovering vices and wondering about the how and the why. Nothing else now. Trying to better understand the reasons and the rites of some friendly figures who were living their own lives very different from the one who had been involved and had nothing to share with spurious children. Or were they legitimate children? It was necessary then for David Mondine to stop and chat with some of them because the progenitor was obscure and far away. Disdaining so that they could thus provide news about a true friend, who had died in Paris.

Gathering information and investigating with generosity. Weaknesses to recognise or protection of some intimacies? Especially in the face of a painful death.

Mário de Sá-Carneiro, in fact!

This was imposed upon him by the devout gratitude and dutiful commitment made to Mr Craston. Thus becoming aware that it was necessary – this is what David Mondine said to himself – to meet some specular and intriguing figures.

Senhor Fernando António Nogueira Pessoa had in fact requested, albeit indirectly, an appropriate investigation.

IV

Rua Augusta. Hotel Frankfurt. Room and board at 1500 réis. Camera alone 350 réis.

David Mondine appeared on the street after exiting the Hotel. He looked right and left. The *Livraria Verol,* just to the right. A large shop window. Books carefully displayed. Also printed on site. Well-prepared publications. Leather covers, gold filigreed spines, refined bindings. A splendid edition of *Os Lusíadas* by Luís Vaz de Camões. Lisboa 1720. In folio. Comment by Manuel Correa.

In the street, meanwhile, a Miranda donkey pulled a cart, harnessed by two rough staves as if they were a sacred yoke. Beating the cobbles with resounding clops. Miserable clothes for sale piled on the bed of the cart. Wretched, filthy goods. Also hopes for a meagre profit. The good grace of other poor people. Muddy used clothes stinking of old sweat, with patches covering rips caused by misuse.

On the ground, along the bases of the buildings, wicker baskets were defiled by worm-eaten fruit and by the secretions of vegetables yellowed by time. A basin held sardines swollen with salt water while wooden trestles displayed pieces of salt cod. On guard, only melancholy glances. Men and women lost in misery.

Further on, the Monumental Arch sat proudly at the end of Rua Augusta. *Antiqua gesta.* Immortalising glories. Signs of histories. Splendour consumed in memories. The memory of a past triumph. Solemn grandeur. Not to forget that there was what there is no longer. Meanwhile, a clock rang out the present time. The statues of the Lusitanian heroes were the pride of a people.

Viriatus[40] in primis, who fought against the Roman legions. Then *Vasco da Gama*, the *Marquis of Pombal* and *Dom Nuno Álvares Pereira*. Dom Nuno was also known as the Santo Condestável. He heroically defended Portuguese independence in the Battle of Aljubarrota. It was 14 August 1385.

Beyond the monumental arch, which seemed to block the view of the Rio Tajo, was a statue of the king *Dom José I* on horseback. A very Catholic and reformer king. José I who was His Royal Highness the Most Serene Infante of Portugal, His Royal Highness the Prince of Brazil, His Most Faithful Majesty the King of Portugal and the Algarves. José did not, however, disdain reaping exorbitant benefits from the colonial economy in Brazil. Immense plantations and hard slave labour. As a royal right, he received one fifth of the gold extracted from the Brazilian mines. Indeed it was necessary that goods of the most profitable businesses ended up in the coffers of the state, since they were of a royal monopoly thanks to the *Companhia Geral de Comércio do Grão-Pará e Maranhão* and the *Companhia Geral de Comércio de Pernambuco e Paraíba.*

Dom José I imposed his authority, opposing also the *Societas Iesu*. He even managed to expel the Society which, with its irresistible influence and its interests, had obscured the royal power and had allegedly participated in conspiracies such as that of the Duke of Aveiro who tried to dethrone José I in 1758. Hence it was necessary to remember Dom José I with a monumental equestrian statue.

Rua Augusta also seemed to be a street of ambitious businesses. The ostentation of a rapidly enriched bourgeoisie. Women especially. Long skirts. Tight bodices. High collars with gold pendants. Shoes with buttons. Velvet hats. Tortoiseshell spectacles. Chantelle lace stoles. Leather gloves with gold buttons. Fans with ivory slats. Silk umbrellas. Hand-painted purses. Fur muffs and collars. Ornaments of excellent workmanship.

40 Lusitanian leader during the wars fought between the Roman legions and the Lusitanian people.

Meanwhile, next to the Hotel Frankfurt, a shop attracted attention. *OLD ENGLAND.* A sign marked with Bodoni characters in an Art Nouveau frame. Forged iron at its best. '*Importação Directa*'. '*Surprehendetes Novitades*'. '*Alfayateria, Camiseria, Gravataria, Luvaria*'. Immobile figures crowded in front of the windows. Annoying chatter. Slyly complacent grins. Exchanging knowing smiles. Cunning glances. Contemptuous toward those piled up along the bases of the buildings. David Mondine turned his eyes away, suddenly remembering the demanding duty to reach a third floor in Rua dos Fanqueiros.

Which streets to frequent? A pleasant route if possible, he said. A nice stroll as well. At a rhythmic pace. Lingering. Lingering. Palaces and monuments worthy of attention. From Rua Augusta to Rua dos Fanqueiros: the ancient Rua da Princesa which had been a busy drapery and woollens market. A short route, if he wished. Better though to take his time. Moving then. Taking cross streets until the Praça Dom Pedro IV. To the Rocio that is. Then Praça da Figueira. Turning then into Rua dos Fanqueiros. A good thing. Maybe even coming across a café. Sitting down. A lovely *vidro* of the harbour. Breathing an air pregnant with *saudade.* Listening to an idiom of deaf tonality, of nasal sounds and obsessive suffixes.

David Mondine then moved straight toward Rua Dos Sapateiros. To honour a promise he made to himself. Impossible not to pay homage, as the 1910 *Baedeker* advised, to the renowned beauty of a building commissioned by the brothers Ernesto and Joaquim Cardoso Correia. The *Animatografo do Rossio* in Art Nouveau style. Open to the public on 8 December 1907. Curvilinear features. School of Victor Horta and Hector Guimard. Architect-artists. Three openings. The box office in the centre and two side entrances. Facade with green carved wooden reliefs. Decorative panels of *azulejos.* The work of José António Jorge Pinto. On the façade, two female figures with braided hair holding steles surmounted by lamps.

Having seen what he had promised himself to see, David Mondine made a quick about-turn. He moved straight for Rua de São Nicolau. He began to quicken his pace to reach Rua Nova do Almada. He then turned quickly to Rua Garrett. He saw two men in a corner who interchanged words with unequal commitment. The one, in a black suit, hat in his left hand, spoke with a terse tone leaving the other to reply only with a *"sim"*, a *"não"*, a *"certamente"*, as he stood timid and sullen fiddling with one end of his white shirt. Quarrels of words and gestures. A messy questioning. A bullying based on status and wealth. So it seemed. *Do ut facias.* One part seemed to succumb. Obedience required. Appropriate then to move away.

Rua Nova do Almada appeared wide. Flashy awnings protecting the shop windows from barely seen rays. High edifices embellished with finely forged iron railings. Symmetrical facades, certainly rebuilt after 1755 when an earthquake touched 8.7/9.0 on the Richter scale. Re-reading the notes from the precious *Baedeker.* Page after page. Dense writing. Disturbing news. Waves of death from a turbulent sea. Also flames from blazes. The victims numbered between 60,000 and 90,000. Divine punishment?

"(God) removeth the mountains, and they know not: which overturneth them in his anger. Which shaketh the earth out of her place, and the pillars thereof tremble." Thus spoke Job[41].

Perhaps a vendetta. Indeed the *indios* had been massacred without *pietas.* The fault of the *"reducciones jesuitas*[42]*"*? So it was said with brazen modesty. Meanwhile, at home, the reconstruction began.

In Rua Nova do Almada the many shops were crowded one against the other. There were many passers-by. Descending and ascending a serpentine pavement. Unstable equilibria. Meanwhile he was busily reading the many signs posted on the balconies. *'COMPANHIA UNIÃO FABRIL,* Limitada – *Rua 24 de Julho nº 940 Lisboa* – ADUBOS CHIMICOS e MASSA DE

41 Bible, Job 9, 5-6.

42 Religious settlements established to control the indios and convert them to Catholicism. The "reductions" were small villages built on a uniform plan, with a central square and church, so as to keep watch over the residents.

PURGUEIRA'... '*POSTAE ILLUSTRADOS* – Manoel Ignacio Roque – *118, Rua do Arsenal, Lisboa*' ... '*ALBERT BEAUVELET* – Agência General de Automóveis – *Palácio Foz – Das antigas cocheriras dos Castello-Melhor, Lisboa*' ... '*NAVALIS* – Sociedade de Construção e Reparação Naval – *Rocha do Condo de Óbidos, Lisboa 3*'.

Mondine stared for some time at those opaque and clumsy writings, forged and marked with doodles that had nothing artistic about them. Epigraphs that seemed designed to induce sadness. *Saudade* reigned. Representations of creative minutia. Nothingness, basically. Simply reminiscences by those capable only of trivial creations. An inadequate style. Why not have entrusted the handwriting to the artistic bizarreness of a José de Almada-Negreiros?

Certainly, one would have obtained a singular feature since a Futurist soul with a disordered para-geometric inclination would have provided signs of singular eclecticism and lively magnificence. Also in Art Nouveau style if one wished, as Almada-Negreiros had done in his designs for *Cunha Taylors* or for *Capa Revista Contemporânea.* Or in sketching in imitation of the silhouettes of Pierrots and Harlequins as he had done for the *Ilustração Portuguesa.* Or playing with features as a cartoonist as he had done in *O Jurnal,* caricaturing the playwright and poet Júlio Dantas.

Dejected, David Mondine headed straight to Rua Garrett. In the intersection was proudly displayed a busy shop, with large windows protected by an Art Nouveau iron canopy, which offered to its clients the *Grandes Armazéns* on the first floor. A few more steps since his intention was to take Rua do Carmo to see up close the terminal part of the *Elevator Ouro-Carmo.* Wrought iron. Neo-Gothic design with four-mullioned windows. Thirty metres high. Now powered by electricity although a steam engine was used in the early years.

David Mondine suddenly halted his quick pace. What? Remembrances drawn from distant memories and from fantastic thoughts. Desired ambiguity? Thus he turned from Rua do Carmo into Rua Garrett.

With some observation, accompanied by a bit of luck, it might be possible to ensure suggestive encounters. Perhaps meeting Fernando António Nogueira Pessoa? He was probably sitting comfortably in the Café A Brazileira, ready to offer and have appreciated some *Bica*[43] and to smoke. A lost gaze? Solidifying friendships, resuscitating them with pleasant alcohol-induced deliria. *Moscatel. Vinho verde. Beirão. Porto. Clarete. Ginjinha. Madeira...* "*Cálice da comunhão / Com brilho que se perdeu! / Comunhão em união / Entre meus sonhos e eu! / Ó cálice tão amado!*[44]". It mattered little. It would have been sufficient that... Perhaps a meeting with ambiguous friends he had to deal with.

Friends sitting, like phantasms, in that café to pass the day and the night if necessary. Well then? Or perhaps Fernando was there alone to imagine objectives or absurdities concerning poetry and the simple philosophy of being a poet?

However, if any of those ambiguous friends had already taken his place at *A Brazileira*, he had certainly done so also to pass the time and to yield to refreshing alcoholic drinks. And had Mário de Sá-Carneiro ever sat in that café? Doubts. Satisfying doubts?

Forbidden, however, to involve Pessoa in the investigations, to bother him, to drag him into memories if he had no desire to recall the past. Peremptory for this purpose were the instructions given by Mr Craston. To undertake the investigations without disturbing Senhor Pessoa with inopportune enquiries. Only superficial investigations which, at the time, seemed to have the flavour of a hoax. Even without thinking about injunctions and invitations, he often had the suspicion that it was merely a false pretext and that Senhor Pessoa did not have a specific interest in that investigation involving a death. Perhaps he was interested in acquiring documents and writings that this Mário Sá-Carneiro might have left, certainly in Paris, as incriminating traces due to particular confidences. A friend who was a

43 Strong coffee very similar to espresso.
44 Fernando Pessoa, Chalice: *"Chalice of my communion / With the lost thing that gleams! / Communion-bond of union / Between me and my dreams! O chalice of love's most!"*

compulsive correspondent would certainly have kept with him the letters he had received. Also traces of private intimacies, of unspeakable confessions.

Among those wieldy thoughts, David Mondine moved straight along Rua Garrett almost as if he wished to repel every evil temptation. He stopped instinctively when he was facing the façade of the *Igreja dos Mártires.* Here was how Lisbon celebrated its Christianity.

It was the king Dom Afonso Henriques who wished to have a chapel erected in that place. The *Baedeker* was an accurate guide. After the earthquake, the church was redesigned by Reinaldo Manuel dos Santos, and hence its '*pombalina*' style. The mixture was heterogeneous and artificial. Late Baroque and Neoclassicism. A massive central body. At the sides, two parts separated by a cornice. Above, a triangular pediment. The bell tower rose at the back.

The crowd of men and women was now unwieldy, marked as it was by the desire for strolling and shopping.

The cafés and the shop windows were gleaming with attractions. Once again signs, many and varied ... 'AGUAS FUENTE NUEVA – *Sancto Ferreira da Costa* – PORTO' ... 'LOTTERIA e ARTICÓS DIVERSOS – *Vendita por Grosso e Varejo –Papies de Fumar*'... 'CASA BANCÁRIA FONSECA, SANTOS & VIANNA – 120 Rua dos Capelliatas – Lisboa – *Compra e Vende Fundas Publicos, Nacionaes e Estrangeiros*' ... A dense muttering and taking note of an address and a name. Certainly useful, especially if that of a distinguished doctor: 'MARCAL DE MENDONCA Medico – *Rins e Vias Urinarias* – Clinica General – *Rua Do Ouro, Lisboa*' or of some manual ready to be used: 'MANUAL de MEDICINA DOMÉSTICA – *Regra de bem viver par conseguir a longa vida – 958 páginas nitidamente impresso, profusamente illustrado, lindamente encadernado em percalina* – ESC. 35$00'.

Amadeu de Souza Cardoso[45] would have taken offence seeing

45 Distinguished Portuguese avant-garde painter. He died of the Spanish flu at only 30 years of age.

those banal figures displayed. Why, he would have wondered, not give a wise aesthetic sense to such trivial writings? Letters placed next to one another without artistic attribution. It would have been sufficient to treat colours and frilly graphic ornaments differently. Pleasing decoration for a city. Also coloured pictorial signs and seductive abstractions. Marking different aesthetic paths. Also highly personal formal solutions. Prevalence of colour over form. It would have been excellent taking inspiration from his "*Mascara de Olho Verde*[46]". Thus rendering good service to those who were walking and distractedly might perceive engaging expressive signs.

David Mondine suddenly found himself, among consuming and thus undesired thoughts, in front of the café A Brasileira – Genuíno Café do Brasil. Walking lightly, almost brushing the ground. Also fears. Fear of dispersing suggestions peppered with tales of memories and memories of tales.

Mr Craston had been explicit when sending the memorandum.

An ambiguous coterie loved to come together in that café. Even though it seemed at that moment that there was only one individual. A coffee, a glass of *Vinho do Porto* and an always-lit cigarette. Spying through the window, marred by writing and filth. Only a silhouette, so it seemed. Where then were Álvaro de Campos, Dr Ricardo Reis and António Mora? Appearing and disappearing at will. Being one or many. The *Vinho do Porto* certainly helped to survive.

Desolate steps. Then moving about desolate streets.

Largo das Duas Igrejas greeted David Mondine with its churches. A rapid pace in crossing the Largo. Just a quick look at the facades. The *Igreja da Encarnação* with its Neoclassical styles peppered with '*rocailles*[47] elements. Significant the devotion to Saint Catherine. The *Baedeker* mentioned it. Indeed, when misfortune struck, one took courage whispering to the rosary what

---

46 The painting represents a mask with one green eye. The face is painted on different planes with bright colours. A typical example of expressionism.

47 Decoration realised in imitation of natural elements.

that saint repeated. *"No state can be kept in civil law in the state of grace without holy justice."*

Then the *Igreja Nossa Senhora do Loreto* characterised by a large statue of the Madonna protected by two angels. Italian marble. Here, in the invocations *"Avé Maria, cheia de graça, / o Senhor é convosco..."* one was often reminded of what Luke the Evangelist had written[48]. *"And Mary said, Behold the handmaid of the Lord; be it unto me according to thy word. And the angel departed from her."*

Reaching then Praça de Camões which the young porter of the Hotel Frankfurt, João Bento, had recommended highly. It had reminded him of an early youth spent squashed amidst a crowd of men who always thronged the square. Legitimate protest, as in November of six years earlier, at the cry *"a greve não para aqui*[49]*"*.

Indeed, Praça de Camões was a place of demands. Conviction and anger. Meeting around the statue of Luíz Vaz de Camões: *"Príncipe dos Poetas de seu tempo. Viveu pobre e miseravelmente e assim morreu.*[50]*"* David Mondine then realised that he was surrounded by hoarse voices and cries meant to specify reasons and desires.

Meanwhile, along the walls of the buildings, other signs were promoting initiatives and products. 'COMPANHIA DOS TABACOSO DE PORTOGAL – *Campo 24 de Agosto 31 – Lisboa*' ... 'HÔTEL DURAND, Praçado Barão de Quintella Lisboa – *Pensão Completa 2400– 400 réis*' ... 'EMPREZA INDUSTRIAL PORTUGUEZA – A Maior e Mais importante Fabrica Portugueza di Metellurgia – *Rua Vasco de Gama – Lisboa*' ... 'CAFÉ MARTHINHO – *Specializado in* TORRADINHAS de MELEÇAS – *Cucine Française à la carte et prix fixe*' ... Other talents would have been able to transform those ordinary signs into pictorial attractions. José Pacheco or Guilherme de Santa Rita? Perhaps both. Distinctive and charming signs. Novel colouristic virtues and

48 Bible, Luke 1, 38.

49 *"the strike does not stop here."*

50 *"Prince of the poets of his time. He lived in poverty and misery and thus he died."*

unique writing. Marking public attractions. Colours prepared with intellectual thirst. Colours that bolstered other colours. Drawing lines with an original manuality. Unmistakable ingenuity. Transmitting emotions.

David Mondine swerved rapidly, retracing his steps and keeping to the left, for Rua da Trindade. The young João Bento's information had to be taken into account.

Who knows, David Mondine wondered as he walked that street lost in thought, if some of the writers who frequented those cafés had ever imagined writing a guidebook of Lisbon.

Perhaps Senhor Pessoa? Certainly since he was one who preached that *"Sim, fique aqui escripto que amo a pátria funda, doloridamente*[51]*"*. Why not take the trouble then to tell, in his own way and without the nuisance of strange friends, about history, monuments and streets in a little book that might bear the title: *Lisbon – What the Tourist Should See* or *Peregrinações em Lisboa*[52]?

David Mondine stopped abruptly, albeit amidst thoughts, now that he had arrived at a splendid building that intersected Rua do Mondo. A suggestion by the young João Bento. One of the most beautiful theatres in Lisbon, he said. The *Trindade* of Senhor Afonso Taveira. Glancing at it from a corner. Facade in three parts, with stone pillars. Below, three arched wicker doors. Above, a lintel bearing the inscription '*TEATRO DA TRINDADE*'.

Praça de Dom Pedro IV, called *Rocio,* then welcomed David Mondine after a steep ascent taken at a slow pace. A quadrangular space surrounded by buildings in *pombalino* and in *manuelino dentellé.* At the centre the bronze statue of Dom Pedro. An imposing monument, 27 metres high. Sitting down then. Some refreshment while admiring the surroundings. Thoughts turning to the fragrance and taste of a white wine. It was suitable to quench the thirst. Adding also a dessert. Banishing a certain languor.

A Brasileira do Rossio hosted him amidst well-arranged and laid tables. The waiters were quick to offer their services.

51 *"Yes! Let it be written that I love my country deeply, painfully."*

52 A guide with this title was written by Fernando Pessoa in 1925.

A glance about meanwhile, waiting for the order to arrive. A glass of *Vinho Verde* and a delicious *pastél de nata.*

In front, framing the square, *Il Tendinha* which was, according to João Bento, the oldest house of the Rocio. There it was possible to drink, again according to João Bento, a *ginginha.* A liqueur made from black cherries. Meanwhile the noise had become deafening. The trams clattering in the square. The Central Station of the *Companhia dos Caminhos de Ferro Portoghese* was also in front. The facade was in Manueline style. Then the *Teatro Nacional Almeida Garrett.* Quick glances then. The *Botequim do Freitas.* The *Arco do Bandeira* in Pombaline style. Next to it the *Tabacco Gusmão,* a *Camiseria,* the imposing profile of the Hotel Metropolis. Finally, the *Farmacia Azevedos Rios* and the *Farmacia Estacio.*

Beside David Mondine, a table – cluttered with two cups of coffee and a carafe of water with a half empty glass – was presided over by a nondescript man reading the *Diário de Lisboa* in a low voice while smoking with annoying ostentation. Every now and then he threw a glance at his neighbour almost as if it were an invitation for a friendly conversation. Pages flipped through with irreverent reluctance. Also folded with noisy aversion. Was he looking for something that might interest him or was he sure that nothing of what was printed could be of interest? Bizarre ambiguity of amusing himself. Practising a presence spent undoubtedly in wishing to exhibit full-blown disquietude. Or so it seemed. All of a sudden, indeed abruptly, that gentleman, facing David Mondine, agitated the newspaper and said, in a tone marked by arrogance: Obscure business, at least so I believe!

– Excuse me?, David Mondine said, turning his head.

With a quick gesture, the man pulled his chair up to David Mondine's table. He settled himself and set the newspaper aside. A man about 30 years old, thin, not too tall, somewhat hunched while sitting but fairly straight when he rose for a moment to adjust his chair. He wore a somewhat wrinkled suit. Slate grey. Grisaille waistcoat with metal buttons. White shirt worn at the cuffs. Ash grey tie. Narrow-brimmed trilby hat. Bamboo walking stick with bone knob. He was pale, with an air of great suffering, almost as if anxiety and worries were devouring him.

– The horrible existence of those who live without other prospects, he said abruptly, and added, – all one can do is to give account to himself of his ambiguous fantasies ... fantasies that often oppress. Bewilderment, then. Something else? Almost phantasms born from ourselves that we want to be part of our lives. Don't you think? The press, in fact, only gives news of inane happenings. But nothing which might be of comfort to the disquietude that bars the mind!

– I'm sorry, David Mondine said clutching his shoulders – but in truth I cannot follow the thread of your discourse.

– Bernardo Soares[53], the man then identified himself, holding out a hand and bowing his head: – assistant accountant at the textile firm Vasques & Co. in Rua dos Douradores ... a quiet place, quiet without doubt ... while all around, in the streets I mean as well as in the office, people move hastily and confusedly, almost artificial characters from lives spent in disquietude and without them having bothered to notice it ... thus, for example, my employer Senhor Vasques, a brusque person but not of bad character, and thus the chief accountant Moreira and the comptroller Borges ... they come and go without being aware of what they do or of what others are doing ... routine ... for that reason I am a man without illusions ... I can say with conviction that I am a solitary orphan ... a prisoner of the phantasms that seem to affirm that in reality they do not even exist... but I think, *ultima spes*, that I can talk and keep accounts with them ... in truth, to confess to you with suffering and with frankness, I am merely a man peeking beyond the window of his office with a bewildered look, without seeing what it is possible to see, if indeed one can manage to decipher what one believes or imagines seeing ... in my spare time, I can also be a sombre annotator of witticisms,

53 Some scholars (cf. Marmion Bur, *Characters, Heteronymy and Mental Distress*, Stratford 1935) have stated that Bernardo Soares was a semi-heteronym of Fernando Pessoa. He was the author of *The Book of Disquiet* which he began to write in 1913.

almost a dark humourist of life who seeks to record impressions almost as if they were the major part of disquietude, almost unique and ultimate signs of affirmed vitality.

– Profound and troubled turmoils?, David Mondine then asked.

– Endless disquietudes ... do you understand what I'm saying? ... Also eluded illusions ... should I confess that I am a victim of misunderstanding? ... No possibility to defend myself against these hardships and adversities ... disillusioned, I abandoned myself to carelessness, negligence, lack of interest ... and in the end? ... how to say it? ... I seemed to discover and thus to understand that each of us is more than one, is a many, is, how to say it?, an endless multiplication of himself ... being more than one ... feeling as if he were in such perilous and clumsy games ... heart wrenching and horrifying visions since one realises that he is so many ... not understanding sometimes that ... yes worse than gazing at oneself in several mirrors simultaneously ... distorted images ... faces and limbs marked by an indefinite yearning ... an innate inability to adapt to the reality of life ... seeing it pass and not understanding why it is passing in that way ... also wondering whether it makes sense that a something, called life, could ever flee in this way ... often without participating in it ... viewing it only with severe critical notes and imagining what it is only possible to imagine ... finally wondering why judge it if you do not accept its existence ... an intricate business since surrounded by constant and inconstant longings, by a quiescent madness ... I have often wondered if, by chance, I'm not merely an unreal figure or if, instead, what is unreal is the reality that surrounds me ... a slothful game that conditions my life ... not being able to know what it is essential to know ... a deliberately equivocal ambiguity so that everyone can become lost in anxious thoughts.

He abruptly fell silent. Then he began to sip water from the half empty glass. He smiled with ill-tempered impudence. He stroked the brim of his hat with exasperating slowness. He adjusted the knot of his tie. He smoothed the lapels of his jacket. Then he moved even closer to David Mondine, awaiting a response from his interlocutor.

– Are you confessing a disadvantaged existence?, David Mondine asked. He was embarrassed. He could not understand why this Bernardo Soares wished to speak with him, discussing the meaning of life, or rather the discomfort of his life which he, David Mondine, did not know at all. To frighten him? Or perhaps he was merely a provocateur. Perhaps an intelligence aimed at trapping others in a subtle intellectual challenge. Perhaps a man who had lost his sense of reason but who conjectured with wise irrationality and surly pusillanimity. Perhaps someone who lived in perennial disquietude because otherwise he would never have been himself. Perhaps someone who belonged to a fictional world. Is that possible?

– Did you ever have the opportunity or the good fortune to meet a certain Mário de Sá-Carneiro, in whose life and whose death I am particularly interested?, David Mondine asked and added: – He was certainly overwhelmed by a profound existential unease very similar to your own, which led him to his death, so I've been told ... perhaps to suicide ... it's difficult to understand the true reasons for such an extreme gesture ... perhaps he was also infected with an annoying and incomprehensible malaise ... I am seeking plausible elucidations concerning his death ... I am carrying out, although I say this with some hesitation, an investigation into his death ... the desire to know events and circumstances ... to analyse if possible ... a funeral march toward a certain truth ... learning facts and events of his life, of his short life ... I am seeking those who had the good fortune to know him or at least to meet him ... I want to understand ... I would be pleased to understand ... I owe it to the friends ... Mário de Sá-Carneiro, then!

– A name not at all new to me, replied Bernardo Soares interrupting. He paused for a few moments. He was thoughtfully silent. He took another sip of water: – Mário de Sá-Carneiro, you said?, then resumed: – ... I heard his name, if I'm not mistaken, in particular circumstances ... was he a poet? ... almost a foolish second-rate poet? ... these are the rumours that were about in such a provincial city as Lisbon ... by chance did he also write some sad books or poems in wishy-washy magazines? ... yes, Mário de Sá-Carneiro!... I have some dim memory ... certainly the vulgar gossip about him ... it was rumoured ... neurasthenia if I'm not mistaken ... there were no illusions about his future ... someone was sure of his inglorious end ... suicide or murder? ... he had tormented himself with the cruellest human weaknesses ... that was the gossip ... someone else, always inconclusive rumours, claimed that he could have had a bright future as a poet ... but he began to visit other lands if I'm not mistaken ... Paris, if I recall ... he undoubtedly had someone who bankrolled him ... the money had to come from his father's pocket ... Mário de Sá-Carneiro? ... a damned kept man, it was gossiped ... he also had a good defender, a soul mate ... at least here at home ... I heard then that he became mixed up in obscure affairs in that Paris of easy women and bistros for cirrhosis ... others derided him because, so it was rumoured, he had become a fat mummy devoid of will ... apathetic ... Mário, Mário de Sá-Carneiro ... perhaps he met his death in a fight with some devious gigolo ... it's what I know ... rumours are true and false at the same time ...

– And the disquietude you were talking about? Do you think that Mário was also afflicted with it?, David Mondine asked.

– It was merely a simple and unique reflection on altered senses ... I don't know if Mário de Sá-Carneiro was prey to such a singularity ... tragedy thus becomes inevitable, said Bernardo Soares suddenly and he added: – A harrowing flow of malevolences without emotionality and imagination ... an obscure malaise ... I would like, forever, to be an individual able to understand what he sees instead of being an individual who understands only that he does not understand what he sees ... only an incompetent vagabond lost in the wicked mind of a waster of life. I no longer want to be myself ... I would like to refer to others the anxieties that torment me ... dissociation of personality? ... indeed I imagined it, but I wondered if that other ego didn't have within itself also a part of my prime ego ... in which case I would have continued to suffer from disquietude due to transitivity ... I also wondered if it weren't the case that I somehow sublimated this immoral disquietude ... a very equivocal speculation ... why in fact imply this impulse? ... within me or without me? ... to escape the anguish by submitting to a different existence? ... it might be plausible but ... here I remain and I am myself because I participate fully in this existence wounded by disquietude and ... I would no longer be myself if I sublimated this impulse ... I am there where disquietude exists ... it could be no different ... thus often I can no longer manage to decipher myself in that mishmash of decisional probabilities ... I am a prisoner of wills which certainly belong to me and which I cannot prevent from being mine because otherwise I would suppress my being ...

– And consciously take hold of the past, lucidly confirm the present and responsibly wish for a future?

– A re-proposal of time ... I would say: a mediation with time, a fruition through time ... do you understand? ... Impossible ... time for me has no meaning and yet ... I have often played with time ... I didn't want to recognise its value ... what value does it have in fact? ... apathetically watching the passage of the hours without knowing what meaning it has ... without any stress I watched others busy in the ambiguous concept of unreasonableness ... I wondered why no one considered it appropriate to yield to starvation ... reserve their being for more unreal destinies in the face of that reality which is not what one believes it to be ... break with oneself when things are imagined that in reality are not so because they are ... in a divided mind ... thus not understanding what the others are saying and doing ... almost an ominously deceitful dream ... becoming used to driving away the iniquities? ... I tried, certainly ... here one is inevitably overwhelmed by anxiety ... by an unhealthy and corrosive disquietude ... by the sublime mystery of life ... perhaps it's this ... only this ...

– The mystery of life and death?

– That is?

– I was given the task of trying to understand the why and how of a foretold death ... Mário de Sá-Carneiro: remember? ... was his death a sly way to affirm his ego? ... perhaps also to exhibit himself in extreme circumstances ... what on earth should I do? ... I accepted a job and I must do it ... in truth I have great difficulty in fathoming the reasons for which ... this is my problem ... my insidious anxiety ... must I perhaps hurt pained and distressing feelings ... rightly I fear myself as inquisitor ... can you ever be a skilled interrogator if you are not aware of your inquisitorial skills? ... sometimes I think that I'm not a good judge, having to decipher the moods of those who desired or suffered death ... it is necessary, in my opinion, to truly know the disquietudes that wound a mind willing to indulge in the harshest disquietudes ... seeking to profoundly understand, in this case, the mind of Mário de Sá-Carneiro in order to ... how to relate then to a troubled man? ... I am still speaking of Mário de Sá-Carneiro ... sounding out friends or acquaintances? ... how can I consider the ambiguities if I must share doubts and perplexities with people who are also afflicted with doubts and perplexities? ... thus I'm overwhelmed by a nostalgic disquietude that does not allow me to be a good investigator ... I wish that ...

– Nothing is more fatal than having nostalgia and thus disquietude for things that may not have ever happened or with people who might not be such ... this could be your case if you did not know the person who tragically ended his life ... with an indecipherable death? The disquietude becomes even more heart-breaking when you are faced with things impossible to understand precisely because they are impossible ... yet death is the only thing certain if you are aware that it is a fundamental stage of so-called existence ... that perhaps might be of use to you.

– And death by suicide?

– God, a suicide! ... An act that gives one perhaps the only escape from disquietude ... we are not dealing with a dreamless sleep, as some believe and babble on about, inspired by Socrates ... you wake up from sleep and find yourself once again facing perpetual anxiety and mournful disquietude ... you don't wake up from death ... perhaps the sleep of bliss ... then disquietude doesn't follow us and no longer catches us ...

– And the friends left behind forever? ... lost perhaps in the drama of disquietude, as you are saying ... there is then the absolute necessity in wanting to understand the reason for such an extreme gesture... of ...

– Extreme? Death is only death ... we are death ... life is a mere illusion ... it's only the painful indolence of what we call existence. Those reposing in death are the only ones who cannot die, and thus are eternal ... are alive in death ... a paradox? ... it's necessary to become accustomed to paradoxes ... it's necessary to be, above all else, intellectually wise ... it's necessary to be sensible because then it's possible to organise external events so that they have as little impact as possible on the disquietude that grips us ... it is very difficult, in truth, to be indoctrinated about this ... a practice which marks existence ... I do not feel disquietude faced with situations so marginal, extreme, dialectically ambiguous ... in fact they do not appear immutable and thus do not mark or corrupt existence itself ... they live their reality outside of the self that created them and that, in some way, suffers from them ... often I try to sharpen my feelings so as to have a way to create in myself an intimate space where I can arrange, at my will, that which I wish to possess and thus live peacefully ... at times I manage to be indifferent to the disquietudes of others ... indeed I must dissolve, above all, my unhealthy disquietudes, my mournful restlessness, my overwhelming trepidation ... only in that way can I understand that others experience, in truth and for me, merely marginal disquietudes compared with my disquietudes which I consider absolute ... unsolvable ...

– Hence it is possible, in your opinion, to accept an extreme act as a solution to an innate disquietude? Or perhaps it's a rewarding expedient as a moment of original steadfastness and of an accepted condition?

– I am not what others think I am ... I am merely an individual who knowingly suffers the intense masochistic pleasure of experiencing, at times, a profound disquietude that is subjected to a weak and arrogant hope ... hope as a kind of myth ... a hope that is inaccessible, unreachable because it is something intangible ... it would not be the same thing if I could face it, dialogue with it, change it with something of hopeful concreteness ... thus one lives in the delicate pleasantness of the imponderable ... for this hopeful illusion we accept, at times, the dark and inscrutable face of disquietude ... desiring a possible hope is not a contradiction to what I told you earlier, to the irrational ignorance in which we are immersed ... to protect ourselves, we set ourselves a goal that may well be a false objective and therefore we believe maliciously that we are taking a redeeming journey ... we do nothing else but deceive ourselves, pretending not to deceive ourselves ... perhaps this is a subtle truth that no one has the courage to disclose and to admit ... indeed what can be more enthralling than to mix the bitterness of disquietude with hopeful gratification ... hence to accept that disquietude so that it can be gratifying? ... thus I gather, or think to gather, on my shoulders the anguishes of the world!, Bernardo Soares finally exclaimed.

Then he abruptly arose almost as if he had become aware of the time that had passed or of unavoidable commitments. He peered at the windows beyond which it was possible to see men and women busily passing by. Existences spent seeking a reason for an inconclusive life? A short bow toward David Mondine and he rushed among the café's tables muttering incomprehensible phrases to himself. At the door, he held up his left arm and waved his hand as a sign of farewell.

V

Rua dos Fanqueiros.

David Mondine descended with rapid steps. Glances aimed at deciphering numbers indicating doors. Stumbling occasionally. Splintered paving stones and a bumpy street. Precarious balance. Also a certain attention required to dodge the hasty passage of men and women. A melee. Elbows used to make one's way when necessary. Unrepentant chattering. Abrupt stops. Friendly congregations. Ominous gatherings. Exchanges of greetings and gifts. A *"bom-dia"* and an *"olá"*. Hats taken off. Glancing at watches. Silver chains. Displaying complacency. Made-up women. Plumed hats. Ample handbags. And gloves. Long gloves despite the heat. Stopping from time to time. Shop windows, of course. Crowds. Entrances clogged. Intrusive and disrespectful comings and goings. Buying things. Looking at the goods and feeling satisfied.

Strolling the high street with tacit sensuality. Slipping along streets filled with hope. Lightly touching. Chattering with a conventional language. Glances that pursued footsteps. Turning to admire. Malicious comments. Amicable fictions. Hypocrisy. Suddenly irreverent pick-pocketings. From the richest to the poorest. Fat wallets changing pockets. Giving an unseemly rich metropolitan bourgeoisie the possibility of inappropriate grumblings. The colonial economy had provided its fruits. Obscure dealings. Building fortunes. The social pyramid was comfortably solid. Impossible to subvert the order. The bourgeois aristocracy and aristocratic bourgeoisie seemed indestructible. Cornerstones to legitimise a republic. The monarchy could just as well die. Fictitious well-being. Proceeding. A *"bom-dia"* and an *"olá"*.

Meanwhile, in the corners of the streets, some tradesmen worked away at very strenuous jobs. Also unpredictable in terms of safety. Piles of filthy garbage to be recovered, swept, picked. Excrement of animals to collect by sweeping amidst the foul stench. The life of street cleaners. Also the life of itinerants, little more. Goods and products of all kinds. Fraudulent scales. Making fun of those who wished to be derided. Getting by on equivocations. Then delivering the goods to homes. Hence baskets of foodstuffs to be delivered over thresholds. Daily deliveries for those who desired not to mix with a roving mob. Reaching the upper floors by way of steep stairs. Affluent people dedicated to starvation or noble entertainments. Swathed in filthy clothes they prepared to deliver orders. Sadness for a miserable endeavour. Paid only a few réis. The purchases were lavish. Often futile. Trade in Rua dos Fanqueiros.

'Abel Pereira da Fonseca – vini Sanguinhal, Omaggio e Valdor'. 'Dragaria Dias – Linho'. 'Comerciante di Lanjara e Fancaria'. 'Esta e a Casa Que mais barato VENDE panos Brancos'.

Only precarious illusions. Excessive to imagine writings made with such graphic signs that could be understood by the poor. Perpetrated deceptions. They just had to accept it. Merchants were merchants. David Mondine then recalled a passage from the Bible. A splendid volume. In the Vulgate. Venturini, Lucae 1734? Calfskin binding. Gilded spine. Hand decorated with details in gold leaf. Text in two columns. Ornate initials. Rigid parchment with the title on a gold frame. Memory did not deceive.

"Et intravit Iesus in templum et eiciebat omnes vendentes et ementes in templo, et mensas nummulariorum evertit et cathedras vendentium columbas.[54]*"*

Suddenly an incomprehensible babbling. Hoarse voices, often

54 Bible, Matthew 21, 12: *"And Jesus went into the temple of God, and cast out all of them that sold and bought in the temple, and overthrew the tables of the moneychangers, and the seats of them that sold doves".*

blessed by mediocre alcohol. Then pack animals pulling jerkily. Also braying. Negligence, in fact. Carts laden with poor foodstuffs. Selling what it was possible to sell, also to other poor people. The neighbourhood was what it was on the ground floors. Domiciles of custodians and porters. Wandering about, along those streets where it was necessary to go, almost without knowing another plausible destination. Seeking an adequate profit. Precarious work.

David Mondine then slowed his pace. Searching slavishly. Also searching anxiously as his eyes rested, distractedly, on the splendid *azulejos* of some buildings. Small polished stones. *'Al az-zulaiŷ'*, in fact. Cobalt blues, jade greens, honey browns and orange yellows. Glazed ceramic tiles. Fantastic weaves set amidst calibrated geometric designs ready to reserve spaces and contours in blinding white. Undoubtedly a Moorish influence. Creator of the *manuelito* and the *pombalino.*

David Mondine suddenly stopped at a door with resolute boldness. Was it the building he was seeking? Three floors to climb. Steep stairs at times, treacherous even because of turns at the landings since they had to provide a broad access to the next ramp. Narrow and dark. Also nauseating odours. Certainly cabbage soups simmered beyond reason. Perhaps handfuls of onions fried in rancid oil. Perhaps mixtures of mince and cod.

Third floor and a bell on the jamb of the door on the right.

An old woman, slightly crippled and poorly dressed, greeted him without saying a word. She looked at him with little interest. Certainly she was waiting for him. Certainly she knew who he was. Certainly she didn't pretend to understand why he was there. She moved her head slightly, indicating a room that opened on the right. Not a word to indicate deference or irritation. She slipped away rapidly, dragging her right leg without embarrassment. Thus she disappeared through a glass door from which came a sickening stench of slop.

A door barely closed. Not bolted.

A worm-eaten wooden door. The antique splendour of the inlay was vanishing. Barely visible traces of ancient handicraft.

Walnut with inlaid borders. Panels with squares contoured and outlined by knurled frames. Here and there traces of wormholes. Beautiful shape of the eighteenth-century lock. Exposed plate. An irregular key *'Old Key Alten Schlüssel Ancienne Clé'*, oddly polished, was on fine show in the lock. A small coloured ceramic knob.

The man who greeted David Mondine through the door sat loosely in an armchair upholstered with a lurid covering patched with pieces of different dull-coloured fabrics cut in large squares. The man's eyes seemed lost in innocent volubility of thoughts that accompanied a worried brow. Bright eyes. Head leaning against the back of the chair. Dangling hands. The slightly bent chest seemed to offer bows to whomever was in front of him.

Not an old man. Almost skeletal. A tight face with features that seemed to consume a fragile bone structure. Olive, almost Middle Eastern, complexion. Bushy eyebrows. Aquiline nose. Thinning hair, slicked back and poorly combed. Beard and moustache, like the index and middle fingers of the right hand, coloured peach yellow, having been irreparably marked by nicotine. He wore a modest grey suit that lacked recent washing and ironing. Worn and crumpled at the knees. He also wore a white shirt with a limp and crumpled collar. Black tie knotted well. From time to time, he nervously passed the fingers of his right hand through his hair and, impassibly letting his hand fall, he stroked his beard with smug delight. He coughed constantly and, at every cough, his throat emitted a harsh mucus-laden reverberation. He puffed voraciously on an almost extinguished cigar and, often and willingly, sucked loudly from a glass filled with an alcoholic mixture. On the ground was a half-empty bottle of *Garrafeira*.

Beside the armchair on which the man was seated was a slate blackboard daubed with formulae and indecipherable signs. Next to the armchair, a beautiful ivory chessboard resting on a wobbly oak table. Certainly eighteenth-century pieces, carved and of rare beauty. Undoubtedly from *Kholmogory*, or crafted in imitation, given the skill with which they were inlaid with walrus ivory. The figure of the king was circa nine-and-a-half centimetres tall. The pawns only reached six cm. Each piece had a side marked by green reflections, while the other side had a natural colour. The kings and queens had carved faces. The bishops were elegantly decorated. The knights rode horses with hooves in relief. The rooks were dome-shaped. The pawns had only slightly formed faces.

The room was small but bright. Two windows displayed the roofs of homes in Rua dos Fanqueiros. The bright red tiles were resplendent. Overly dazzling, as the sun seemed to create chromatic refractions. Alternately lights and shadows. Also enchanting chiaroscuros. Meanwhile, upon a quick glance, the room seemed divided into heterogeneous corners. Piles of well-selected papers. Here letters, there newspapers. Elsewhere twisted and clipped sheets that hosted cryptograms, puzzles, charades, synonyms, anagrams, syllabic antipodes and palindromes. There seemed to be a stubborn propensity to conserve scraps of paper of any size and colour. A passion that seemed to be consumed in the desire to surround himself with puzzle magazines which, in some way, had meaning by their content, their palpability and their chromaticity. Living mystically, breathing odours of printed papers or those impregnated with black, green or red inks. Meanwhile, dust and ashes were constant, annoying presences. The environment seemed unhealthy, but well lived in. Certainly comfortable for the person who occupied it.

The man raised his head.

He peered at David Mondine for a few moments and with a faint voice said: – I am Dr Abílio Quaresma ... a doctor without patients, but a practical decipherer of enigmas according to those who turn to me to untangle mish-mashes. It is rumoured that I am even able to solve criminal or simply illegal questions, or intricate mathematical and chess problems because, and it's true, I can perceive reality in its deepest essence freed of annoyances and unsettlements ... I must confess without fear that subtle and selfish intentions and an exasperating ambition consume me ... almost the need to satisfy the primal sense of life ... nothing is more daringly complacent, engaging and comprehensive than … the determined understanding of heinous actions, of ambiguous behaviours and of bloodthirsty acts which, at first glance, may seem impossible to resolve … in truth they are elementary enigmas if examined with clear rationality … do you understand what I mean? … indeed, nothing can be more satisfying than deciphering enigmas that seem to have no solution … an exciting and lustful mental complacency … ambiguously playing and juggling with the obstacles that mark our lives and those of others … becoming excited until I manage to find the solution to a specious abstrusity, a clumsy deceit, a bizarre puzzle … it is true intellectual masturbation … do you understand, my friend? … it's not hard to understand … forgive my verbose chatter … I don't receive many visits so … here we come to you … you are? … Well, if memory serves me well, you must be the distinguished Lieutenant Arthur Hastings … or am I wrong?

– Arthur Hastings?, David Mondine asked.

– The collaborator of Hercule Poirot, I mean … or rather a friend, as Monsieur Poirot often dares state *"a friend who for many years never left my side. Occasionally of an imbecility to make one afraid, nevertheless he was very dear to me*[55]*"* … I would say instead that he is one of his illustrious collaborators … yes, exactly an illustrious collaborator of that ill-mannered little man, of that ex-inspector of the Belgian police, of that small man, less than five feet three inches tall, plump, self-centred, vain, not at all jovial, with a curious egg-shaped head, with that very amusing moustache and who babbles about being the world's best detective and who also monotonously repeats that *"murder is a habit"* … but a habit of what? … *consuetudo delinquendi?* … a presumed or confirmed habituality? … perhaps social? … I am opposed to that unjust premise … a subtle death wish? … perhaps it is Monsieur Poirot who, having to absolve himself from an unconscious sense of guilt, feels the need to state that *"murder is a habit"* without explaining whether it is a habit to practise it or to discover

55 Agatha Christie, *The Murder of Roger Ackroyd.*

it ... yes, Monsieur Poirot who, as a very frivolous and obsessively methodical man, is the protagonist of the strange and intricate mish-mash that was *The Mysterious Affair at Styles*[56] ... therefore, I was expecting, with a certain ironic worry I must confess, Lieutenant Hastings ... it is clear that I mistook the day and time ... indeed it was Lieutenant Hastings who asked for the meeting ... he is, in fact, somewhat perplexed about Monsieur Hercule Poirot's way of acting and his conclusion regarding *The Mysterious Affair at Styles.* Lieutenant Hastings believes that Monsieur Poirot has somehow wrongfully cheated so as to provide a reliable and plausible solution to the mystery ... murder is a habit, remember ... a bad affair, an unseemly matter ... and that occurs often, believe me, when one has the belief that one's intuition, and Monsieur Poirot counts especially and comprehensively on his unfailing intuition, is a special detector for a solution regarding a murder. But you are?

– David Mondine ... charged by the Henderson & Craston Detective Agency of London to investigate the death of Mário de Sá-Carneiro. I was urged to meet with you to ask for your help with the investigation, said David Mondine and quickly added: – It is an obscure matter, as you well know ... it is necessary however to reassure in some way Senhor Fernando Pessoa who, despite having received a letter from his *amigo de alma* in which he wrote, it was the thirty-first of March, that he would have taken a strong dose of strychnine and would have left this world forever, desires a thorough investigation of what was written by Mário de Sá-Carneiro and that nothing else, if not the suicide foretold in that letter, had been the true cause of his premature demise.

– Ah, now I remember ... of course I remember well ... Mário de Sá-Carneiro, of course! ... Fernando Pessoa's *amigo de alma*, undoubtedly! ... an intriguing affair as I recall ... unpleasantly intriguing ... an event of a few months ago, correct? ... a dilemma not easily resolved at first sight ... suicide or not suicide? ... free

56 Agatha Christie's first detective novel.

oneself of something or be freed? ... an interesting proposition in his enigmatic and ambiguous contrivance ... what can I say? ... a fascinating dilemma that seems not to admit a plausible solution at first glance ... an affair that perhaps must be settled with appropriate investigations ... perhaps! ... I would say almost a mathematical puzzle to tell the truth ... an illogical mystery because there is the need to understand the conclusion of an act that has already happened ... basically it is the act itself that is interesting ... the act as a final solution ... but what act? ... what meaning must one attribute to that act? ... going back then to the moments that caused the act? ... knowing intentions, situations, states of mind ... as if ... well ... applying oneself philosophically in regard to that event ... do you know what I mean? ... perhaps it would be appropriate to untangle everything through mathematical formulae capable of untying this inextricable knot? ... it's hard to explain ... a concatenation of facts which then are merely premises for a theorem ... I thought then ... perhaps ... yes, I was thinking of Monsieur Henri Poincaré[57]... do you think he might be of some help? ... I often avail myself of his basic pronouncement ... do you know his saying? ... *"classification of dimensional varieties"*... varieties of actions I might add ... generally this means the learned and insinuating ability to create a list containing all the possible and imaginable varieties but without repetition ... thus it might be possible to obtain, as a final result, a classification to define a function, among intervals that are very close to one another and able to model the intuitive and primal idea when faced with any other subsequent function, or rather with a necessary conclusion ... yes Monsieur Poincaré ... Monsieur Poincaré had the merit to define axioms to give substance to his principle ... I believe that I can demonstrate the validity of what I have just stated and what could perhaps be helpful to us when we might have inherent difficulties

57 Mathematician, theoretical physicist and philosopher, Poincaré (1854-1912) is considered to have had an encyclopaedic mind because he excelled in all the fields of knowledge of his time.

in providing a plausible solution to the case ... to clarify I refer to what specifically is demonstrated in this mathematical formula ... And he nodded at a blackboard on which appeared in large letters an esoteric formula: *n homotopically equivalent to the n-sphere if n = 3. But n > 3 and n > 4.*

– Therefore, in your opinion, might Monsieur Poincaré's formula be useful to comprehensively examine the case concerning the death of Mário de Sá-Carneiro?, David Mondine asked, with inscrutable misunderstanding and convinced scepticism.

– It might if ... perhaps too many ifs? ... but they are inevitable ... as I said: it is a dilemma that may seem almost insoluble at first glance ... just conjectures ... will they be sufficient? ... perhaps it is necessary to make an excursus on analytical psychology and it is not simple ... I say: an intrigue of sentiments determined by emotional relationships? ... possible ... probable ... what then? ... returning to Monsieur Poincaré, we can mathematically relate everything to that *unicum* that Monsieur Poincaré calls a sphere ... only the sphere, as an ideal geometric form, Monsieur Poincaré stated, is characterised by connectivity ... that is by a defined itinerary that can be contracted until it becomes a point because it was and is the only order of the dimensional varieties ... it seems to me that, in our case, we have circles of associates and friends similar to spheres ... a concatenation of friends and of so-called heteronyms ... Fernando Pessoa – Álvaro de Campos – Ricardo Reis – António Mora – Mário de Sá-Carneiro and, once again, Fernando Pessoa ... a relationship that could be interpreted as a circle which, precisely because of absolute sentiments have in themselves a spherical dimension and characteristic. Therefore, as an applied conceptual tool it could be the final point of an accredited solution of the enigma ... the solution concerning the death of Mário Sá-Carneiro ... thus Monsieur Poincaré's principle might come in handy ... remember then, and it is important, that only reasoning is a true and unique talent for solving enigmas ... I want you to fully understood my statement ... intuition is frustrating ... a half-empty glass that wishes to appear full ... the truth of a criminal act can be revealed only through purely rational thinking without recourse to other petty artifices ... certainly not by means of theosophy, sensationalism, Paulism or intersectionism, etc. ... all theories now very much in vogue in Portugal ... it is necessary to rely on a rationality capable of accepting the challenge and which allows one to elucidate and investigate the mechanisms of other people's thoughts far better than is possible through common language ... you know this, don't you? ... the solution of an enigma is only a joyful rational challenge ... in this way I have solved cases that seemed difficult to solve ... do you know them? ... *the Vargas case ... the stolen parchment ... the theft of the Quinta das Vinhas ... the case of the triple lock, or the theft at the Banco de Galicia* ... it is always necessary to root out the real cause that determined the incident ... to determine the facts ... then it is necessary to compare them ... as he who has created or determined the enigma (which can also be a criminal act) versus he who undertakes to solve the enigma ... a presumed intelligence versus another intelligence ... the subtle exercise of a rational logic versus the illogical atrocity of a criminal enigma ... the mechanisms involved in this clash are many and ... involve a series of components not to be underestimated ... also psychology ... it means knowing the other's way of acting, the other's behaviour, the reasons why the other acts and moves in a certain way ... certainly not through hyperbolic witticisms and grotesque surprises, as Monsieur Poirot does or thinks he does ... concerning the case of Mário de Sá-Carneiro, it is necessary to move with shrewd rationality ... to visit some places ... to go ... to investigate ... to listen to testimony ... to check times ... to read documents ...

– To Paris, no doubt!, David Mondine interrupted.

– Paris?

– Your availability, I was told, is already attested, quite evident I would say ... a necessity that I cannot possibly do without ... I will investigate with tenacity and good will ... it is the task with which I have been entrusted as an official assignment ... when I leave I will undertake to meet and listen to Álvaro de Campos, Dr Ricardo Reis and António Mora ... not Fernando

Pessoa who, as you certainly know, will not wish to be bothered ... I will then report to you on the meetings and confidences ... however, it will be absolutely necessary that you be present in Paris, where I will have to go ... the solution of our case is there ... in Paris ... hence it is necessary to visit, as best possible and with wisdom, the scene of the misdeed ... the place where Mário de Sá-Carneiro met his death ... to sound out those who knew him or, merely and by chance, met him ... those who had the fortune to be close to him in the hours before his death ... who found the body ... who ... in short, all those who might be of help ... you will only have to analyse reports with your confirmed method ... with your reasoning applied to the enigmatic pleasure that involves the solution to the mystery ... you will not have to move about, I assure you ... it will be sufficient that you remain wherever you wish: even in a bistro on the Seine if you desire ... French wines and liqueurs are excellent: as you well know ... Burgundy or Bordeaux: as you wish ... then you can sit in a café and wait for my reports ... I'll punctually report to you what I have learned during my investigations ... I have been well informed of your inveterate and determined habits: you love to solve enigmas while sitting comfortably and thus you dedicate yourself to the study of the crime by gathering information, listening and speaking, and formulating solutions ... or better, defining the only solution ... you can then, when you deem it appropriate, offer me suggestions and give me indications to this purpose so that you can in the end, after we have collected all the necessary information and reports, come to a convincing conclusion ... at least I hope so ... there is above all to ascertain the cause of death ... suicide or not ... and whatever else determined, directly or indirectly, the death of Mário de Sá-Carneiro ... Senhor Pessoa counts specifically on your excellent investigative skills and knows well that, as is your custom, you do not have any thirst for justice but rather the inestimable desire to decipher a mystery ... which is an intricate game of logic ... a formal logic that can become, in the game of mental elaborations, pure mathematical logic ... I believe and I think that you adhere to absolutely reliable practices and that mathematical language, as far as I seem to understand, is the only one that can define a true and coherent consistency in the exercise of logical thinking ... I like to believe that you well understand what I have just stated ... the search for a kind of single truth ... I allow myself to be lulled by the illusion that such truth can provide us with great satisfaction ... a logical and pertinent sequence ... word–thought–idea–argument–reason, in fact! ... so that the truth, the only truth, being something purely subjective and depending on our considerations, can be a single and certain conclusion of each logical sequela ... a valid confirmation of all the deductive argumentations proposed, examined and finally interpreted ... understanding the absolute and unconditional value of that procedure ... do you agree?

Abílio Quaresma looked around. Then he focused his attention on the chessboard in front of him: – Do you play chess?, he asked.

– Chess?, replied David Mondine, surprised.

– True logic lives in the game of chess ... understanding the development of a chess game is a refined and subtle detective game ... understanding the moves that players have made or make during a game is equivalent to sharpening inquisitive wills and allowing one's mind to practise the same obscure thoughts that lead to a move by an opponent ... above all, a very healthy drink and a good cigar bolster one's talent to untangle problematic abstrusities ... essential to justify to oneself the existence of time and of life which can be, if well understood, an absolute truth rather than an intuitive misunderstanding ... take example from me, from my way of life, from my exercise of existence, from my bodily indolence ... at the moment I have been here for several days, with a good bottle of port and a few boxes of Peraltas cigars, forgetting even for a moment Poincaré's useful conjecture as mental culture, only to reconstruct, step by step, a memorable and matchless chess game which is a sure guide to wind one's way through the maze of apparent incomprehensibility ... of a crime if you please ... of a crime consumed in ambiguous circumstances ... here: Akiba Rubinstein against Gersz Rotlewi ... a mad genius against a young man of great hopes, already afflicted, as shown by his slender appearance, by a presumed and lethal tuberculosis ... one of the best games of chess ... it was then that a peculiar combination by Akiba Rubinstein was called *"immortal"*... have you ever heard of Akiba Kiwelowicz Rubinstein, my dear Senhor Mondine? ... despite suffering from anthropophobia and psychotic hallucinations, Akiba Kiwelowicz Rubinstein was the inventor of respected and superb opening variations ... extraordinary moves against the Tarrasch defence, such as the 'Queen's Gambit Declined' ... also the creator of the 'Meran Variation' which fundamentally altered the 'Queen's Gambit chess opening' ... these are just some of his many admirable and impromptu chess inventions for which he is remembered as the man who revolutionised the game of chess through surprising and astonishing intuitions, through incredible mental concentration, through a calculational will essential to the needs of each move ... Akiba Kiwelowicz's moves replied instinctively to every move by his opponents without abandoning decisiveness and determination ... it was the subtle logic produced by a mind able, in a necessary instantaneousness, to evaluate the context and apply the knowledge in relation to that context ... which he called deeply structured thinking ... always able to be assisted by keen mental organisation ... to rely also on logic as an act by which the mind can clearly grasp banal truths of simple natures, as the great Descartes put it ... able to consider all the deductive schemes he had mastered, through logic and memory, which were unequivocally inspired by mathematics ... but returning to your request ... what can I say? ... it is impossible for me to torment myself in the study and analysis of an intriguing game such as this ... every move is a proposed enigma which must be understood ... I am dealing with high intelligences confronting one another, intelligences which merit understanding and study ... memorable performances of unique intellects which clashed, but which understood and admired one another ... each one knew the other and well knew what might or might not be the next move ... they mentally assessed the probabilities and were ready to counter any probability ... therefore the match between Akiba Rubinstein and Gersz Rotlewi defined an era and showed the indefinability of all deductive reasoning ... it is pure logic, almost indecipherable ... hence there remains my commitment and desire to study it in great detail because it allows me to understand and study the mechanisms of thinking better than I could ever do by reading manuals ... I need to practise by endlessly repeating that game ... going over the game of deceptions ... the treacherous desires to put the opponent in difficulty ... the incredible sorties able to invent unexpected countermoves ... I have the urgent need, therefore, to weigh every move made by Akiba Rubinstein and by Gersz Rotlewi, each certain strategy used ... each enigmatic complexity ... nothing could ever compel me to leave my exploratory investigation ... come to Paris? ... perhaps ... I think, to satisfy you and not to disappoint Senhor Fernando Pessoa, that this might, I say might, be possible on one condition ... a possible and probable condition ... to bring with me a portable chessboard to ... indeed I believe that the commitment to study the moves of this match would be very beneficial to my intuition so that I might have greater probabilities of solving the enigma facing us ...

Abílio Quaresma said this with great emphasis. Then he was silent. He poured himself a drink. An abundant drink. He fell back limply in the chair. He reached out to take the box of Peraltas. He lit a cigar, inhaled with pleasure and began to stare at the chessboard.

David Mondine walked quietly out of the room.

VI

Aveiro a Beira Mar.

A refreshing locale to establish a meeting. *A Taverna do Lucas.* A necessary pause after a long, tiring journey. Tramway, trains and coaches. Also sudden, almost stifling heat. Inevitable perspiration. Dry throats placated, during brief stops between exhausting transfers, with spring water or with seemingly seductive wines. Whites or reds they may have been. *Madeira Verdelho* or *Quinta do Noval,* or *Vinho Verde Albariño,* or *Monsoon?* Certainly not quality wines. They seemed extracts of hasty, adulterated vinifications. Poor quality. Then the accompaniment. Bread with a stew of *ensopado de borrego*[58] and *azeitào*[59] cheese. Prudently filling the travel baskets to soothe stomachs. Purchases made along the journey to satisfy a hunger that had soon become indecent. Indeed travelling along the Atlantic stimulated the appetite. The sea air, it was said. *Cibi sacra fames*[60].

Then, from above, David Mondine spied the obstinate Cabo Carvoeiro, there in the Peniche, with its *'Pedra da Nau'* which seemed to arise from the sea like a rocky Venus. Beyond the windows, filthy from past rainfalls and filamentous soot, was a bright red of shady oleanders bent upon themselves: bent by a caressing breeze. Thus the red of flowers was intertwined with a bright, rough green of the leaves in the frame of a sky that seemed clear and polished. From

---

58 Dish of meat with onions, chopped garlic, bay leaf, parsley, mint, paprika, chilli pepper arranged in layers and then cooked. Served on slices of fried or toasted bread.

59 Soft sheep's cheese.

60 *Execrable hunger for food.*

time to time, sticky cobwebs embroidered the angles of the cars. Suddenly bothersome bites. Certainly bed bugs, hidden in the folds of the rough ochre-toned upholstery. Nauseating odours of sweat and bread soaked in rancid oil. After turning inland away from coast, there suddenly appeared Vallado, on the Rio Alcoa.

The coach was unsteady, indeed swaying, very old. The roads were dusty and full of potholes, raising cough-inducing clouds. Wicked jolts of the passenger compartment so that one bumped into one's neighbours during the ride. And then the heat. Annoying sweat beaded the faces so that the discomfort had become unpleasantly untoward. Thus Alcobaça was reached, amidst significant inconvenience, for a scheduled stop-over. Alcobaça among vineyards and fruit trees. A little leisure time to visit the *Mosteiro de Santa Maria*, but in haste. Just a while to stretch the legs but no time to waste in visiting the *Mosteiro*. Enough, said the coach driver with sour obstinacy, to admire the splendid facade for a few minutes. The rest could be enjoyed from a distance and with a fleeting glance at pamphlets and postcards purchased as a duty imposed by unwritten rules. A custom practised with determination. Here then the statues, the two towers, the battlements of the side walls and the external apse with its eight flying buttresses. One imagined so, since it was written with learned words in thin booklets for travellers. A tattered *Baedeker* laid down the law in culture. The imagination then became proven reality while a frugal meal was consumed accompanied by watered down wines.

Then David Mondine returned to travelling over bumpy roads in a sleepiness caused by the rocking of the coach and by the meal. After several kilometres, he reached O Cabo Mondego, there in the Serra a Boa Viagem, which proudly displayed a 15-metre lighthouse. Continuing along the coast and changing coaches while retaining discomforts, he reached Aveiro, a town of salt works and lagoons. And there he abandoned the coach and proceeded quickly to the arranged destination.

Despite the exhaustion of a treacherous journey, David Mondine hastily negotiated Largo Luís de Cyprian Coelho de

Magalhães, which was a marketplace. He crossed one of the two bridges over the Ria and, bearing right, found himself in Rua Jose Estevao which was sheltered by broad banks bordering a large lagoon. Along the Canal das Piramides and the Canal Central appeared the coloured *molicerios* with arched pine prow, moved by sails or pulled by tow ropes. The boats seemed to extend to the horizon when in truth they were contained within a mordant cordon of dunes. In this small hemicycle, the lagoon fishing was fruitful and plentiful. Hence the many fishing lines with barbed hooks beyond the parapets of the bridges and along the Côjo quay. Darting fish were easily caught in the barely stirring waters closed within the basin. Meanwhile, the bottom pregnant with mud gave birth to spirals of very fine sand.

The door of the *café-restaurante* opened across from the bridge over the Ria. One entered through a lovely wooden entrance painted sky blue.

David Mondine glanced at his surroundings, seeking the man with whom he had arranged a necessary meeting by means of pressing and garbled telegraph messages.

Would it have been beneficial to consider what it was possible to obtain from an encounter with a person whom some deemed, wrongly or rightly, of uncertain and ambiguous personality? It was difficult to understand the why and the how of such an unscrupulous judgment. Only slanderous ambiguity? The distrust was great. Nonetheless, it seemed inappropriate and scandalous to neglect Fernando Pessoa's indefinable and mysterious friends.

The man awaiting Mondine was settled in a corner next to a large window from which he could observe the comings and goings on the streets and, at the same time, keep well in view the entrance to the place. He had a large tray before him which he watched greedily. Pieces of barely nibbled cheese. Certainly *Queijo de Castelo Branco*, yellowish and slightly crumbly and creamy. Next to the tray a half glass of red wine.

The man slowly stood up as soon as he saw David Mondine approaching him and nodding his head. A slight bow and a whisper: – Álvaro de Campos, he presented himself.

He was a rather tall man. Five feet nine inches, no doubt. He was wearing a coat with a dense row of buttons. A pocket showed a neatly folded handkerchief. The tie had a half-Windsor knot showing – unusual but appropriate precision. Even deliberate ostentation. The shirt was white with a wing-collar. The homburg hat was resting on a chair so that the man displayed straight hair with a side parting. His face was clean-shaven and typical of a Portuguese Jew. A monocle lent a reflexive austerity to the expression of his face.

David Mondine shook hands and sat down opposite him.

– Do you know why I demanded, with inopportune insistence, that we meet in this dive in Aveiro?, Álvaro de Campos asked, with a light-hearted accent.

– In your messages, you told me about a certain food ... an absolute delicacy that it was appropriate to try, almost as if a symposial complicity might give our meeting a less austere, perhaps friendly, form. I'm curious to taste your culinary guile, to which I will succumb driven by a bizarre interest that relies mainly on my predilection for unknown and ethnically surprising dishes.

– Someone who is not Portuguese, like you, undoubtedly deserves a similar reward after such a long and uncomfortable journey ... what is more appealing than enjoying unusual delicacies: true? ... here: *tripas a moda do Porto*!, exclaimed Álvaro de Campos with a satisfied presumption and added: – Not any banal tripe ... but tripe in the manner of Oporto which is another thing entirely ... such that I have in mind a poem that exalts and defines how and when it must be savoured because it is similar to love, or perhaps it is love itself, and he began to recite: "*Um dia, num restaurante, fora do espaço e do tempo, / serviram-me o amor como dobrada fria. / Disse delicadamente ao missionário da cozinha / que a preferia quente, / que a dobrada (e era à moda do Porto) nunca se come fria*[61]", after which he calmed down and added, smiling

61 *"One day, in a restaurant, outside of space and time, / I was served love like cold tripe. / With delicacy, I told the emissary from the kitchen, / that I preferred it hot, / since tripe (and it was Porto style) is never eaten cold."*

slyly: – … I invited you to this restaurant because it is famous for the care with which the dish is prepared … and cooked according to an ancient and respected recipe … nothing is tastier or more refined … the fundamental principles observed … a chicken cut into small pieces, onion, black pepper, cumin, to which is added white beans … finally, a necessary touch … a splash of *Xeres*, sherry made from the palomino grape … what is essential however is the main ingredient … veal tripe with pig's head and ears … for my taste and for your fate, I had the audacity to order two dishes accompanied, it seemed appropriate to me, by a red *Burmester* from the vineyards of the hills embracing the Douro, between Villareal and Villarinho. Agreed?

– Excellent!, exclaimed David Mondine as they took their seats opposite one another and a waiter was preparing to serve them: – as you mentioned, a long journey should be rewarded with a tasty local dish, and he added, – … then you … but I think you are … forgive me but it is Mário Sá-Carneiro about whom I wish to talk, perhaps to bore you … it's for that reason that I asked to meet you … I'm interested in particular about Mário's childhood and youth … periods often not taken into consideration and which instead … parents and more … also the grandparents if they had an influence on his education … childhood friends et cetera … it is Mário de Sá-Carneiro that I really wish to hear about … it's the main reason why I wished to talk to you who are, so to speak, one of the friends most intimately linked to Fernando Pessoa who was, in turn, an *amigo de alma* of Mário.

– Yes, Mário!, exclaimed Álvaro de Campos with a slight trembling of his voice. He smoothed the lapels of his jacket. He tightened his tie, and then added: – Yes, Mário … yes, the friend Sá-Carneiro … I have even taken the trouble to pay homage to him with some verses … a necessary and appropriate recognition … he deserved it on account of the depth and sumptuousness of his poetry … a charming cascade of words … going far beyond any silly notion of traditional poetics … creating poetry through unique suggestions … do you understand? … almost an intimate need … a necessity to grant him majestic recognition …

I was aboard a ship when that irreparable incident occurred ... I was sailing towards seemingly unknown places ... and on board, when we were in the Suez Canal, his remembrance became a magnificent memory ... thus I began to consecrate him ... a poem ... later published in *Orpheu* ... do you know the magazine *Orpheu*? ... the poem was called *Opiário* ... here are some significant verses that honour Mário: *"This life on board is killing me / My head has been feverish for days / Although I look at who is sick / I find no reason to adapt"* ... evasive poetry? ... not at all, only delicately elegiac ... Mário aboard his life ... daily unhappiness ... no reason to delight ... around him also other people were experiencing his suffering ... distinctive sensations ... to escape that oppressive feeling of tedious boredom ... to flee and escape the monotony of a life devoid of true passions, of stimulating desires, of desired negligences ... a poem, in short, dedicated to those who, like Mário, were consumed in a corrosive existential fever ... who were unsuited to life ... who wished to be unsuited to life ... I had a wise and esteemed teacher who taught me to experience life ... I'm talking about Alberto Caeiro from whom I learned a certain controlled mental order even in the delirium of living and creating poetry ... so-called futurist odes full of gnosiological bursts ... thus organically rejecting any philosophical praxis ... And Mário? ... in truth I don't know in what way he had imagined he might escape from this monstrous, boring, dull and slothful reality ... what roads to follow? I have often wondered ... how to endure the corrosive restlessness of his soul? ... I chose to be remembered as a rebel poet ... simply rejecting metaphysics as a redeeming choice ... stating with conviction that the meaning of things has no meaning ... in essence, I have an anomalous vision of the idolatry I profess ... what idolatry? ... this is the feeling that, for me, is everything ... just as it is without adding anything determined, for example, by thought ... yes exactly thought which, in my opinion, is merely a disease ... a feverish disease ready to distort the surroundings, the world I mean which is ... which is merely a projection of sensations.

– And Mário with his sensationalism[62], with his open adherence to some futurist spirit?, asked David Mondine dropping onto his plate the fork that had just harpooned juicy pieces of tripe a waiter had served. Variegated colours in respect of ancient gastronomies. Arab above all. Many spices. Strong, penetrating fragrances. Redeeming essences so that one could obtain the best in the preparation of sauces. An appetising and substantial broth that accompanied savoury sauces. The tripe governed an obscenely luscious dish.

– It was essential to the profound relationship that bound him to Fernando, Álvaro de Campos said, while David Mondine succumbed to the gustatory stimuli of his palate: – what sensationalism asserts, in an incontrovertible manner, added Álvaro de Campos: – ... that is, the original elements of reality seemed to derive exclusively from colours, from sounds, from space, from time, and so on ... in a sort of movementism projected into the future ... but to what I just said I must appropriately add, for your knowledge, that I never met Mário de Sá-Carneiro, Álvaro de Campos said firmly: – yet he was a close friend of mine ... older than me by only five months ... I was born in October 1890 ... Mário in May ... I in Taveira, in the Algarve, a land of Moorish charm, and Mário in Lisbon, in the sprawling capital ... meanwhile our mutual friend Fernando Pessoa was always a fraternal umbilical go-between for Mário and me ... indeed as he was for everyone ... Mário was like a brother, never a putative son, and this should be kept in mind, even though, in my opinion, he needed a father ... his father, Carlos Augusto de Sá-Carneiro, was to be considered a failed father ... even if he felt, because he was a young widower, the need to cavort ... I am reporting what I learned from mutual friends ... also from Fernando ... it is my duty to tell you that if I had personally known Mário ... Mário, certainly! ... unfortunately I was not a valuable substitute ... I tried to tease him with verses ... I quote again from my *Opiário*: *"É por um mecanismo de desastres, / Uma engrenagem com volantes*

62 Literary movement proposing *"sensation"*, *"sensation in all manners"*.

falsos, / Que passo entre visões de cadafalsos / Num jardim onde há flores no ar, sem hastes[63]"... perhaps I wanted to be the brother he never had! ... the impossible father... what else to transmit to him if not the nausea and resignation of life through poetry? ... assumption of a personal failure ... yes: I offered myself as a man melancholically charged with an unwieldy burden of disappointments ... Mário often seemed to be an excellent travelling companion ... Fernando told me about his childhood and I ... I made the commitment not to violate such confidences ... a cruel childhood... governed by the obsessive presence of death ... since his mother had definitively abandoned him ...

– ... an abandonment that caused such great despair?, interrupted David Mondine.

– it was inevitable if you investigate the tempestuous and passionate solitude that gripped Mário ... his misanthropy ... something else? ... an obsessive man who lived life in search of an identity that seemed to escape him ... who was seized by the compulsive desire to investigate the madness that seemed to inexorably consume him ... but was it madness? ... again and again when he was investigating psychological flaws, emotional neglect, his sexuality ... he was a man in prey to an annoying and angry revulsion at everything he believed was mediocre, usual, slothful ... then to find himself, after experiencing profound disappointments, at the mercy of a spasmodic and aggressive aspiration to acquire different, heterogeneous forms of knowledge ... thus precipitating into corrosive, unreal hallucinations, completely devoid of a compliance with real life ...

– ... to thus be dragged toward a dark end?, David Mondine asked with reluctant melancholy.

– But that end could also be considered a supreme act of courage ... let us remember that the profound meaning of life is legitimately peculiar to each of us ... poetry often helps or horrifies ... that is for certain! ... Mário was, in my opinion, a restless

63 *"It is by a mechanism of disasters, / A gear with false fly-wheels, / That I pass into visions of gallows / In an garden where there are flowers in the air, without stems".*

wanderer just as I was ... but that's another story ... didn't you want me to give you my considerations of Mário? ... what more can I say than I've already written in *Opiário*? ... I am talking about Mário, only about Mário, Mário de Sá-Carneiro, in fact ... a biography in verses ... listen ... – he suddenly fell silent. Only for a few moments. He sipped his wine. Then he savoured a *congèrie* of tripe, beans and condiment. Moments later, he nibbled at a smidgeon of offal, accompanying it with another sip of *Burmester.* Álvaro de Campos then sighed satisfied, and he began to recite in a slow, lilting voice:– *"Sou um convalescente do Momento. / Moro no rés-do-chão do pensamento / E ver passar a Vida faz-me tédio*[64]*"*... to say? ... to examine? ... to analyse? ... living beyond contingency ... this is our reckless fault ... also Mário's fault ... perceiving what may be real and concrete for others with very different eyes ... suffering ... enduring ... expiating this virtuous anomaly ... are they or are they not life? ... then: difficult to understand for those who do not accept these considerations ... antinomy ... what really is life? ... what am I in relation to life itself ... is life within me or without me? ... do I have a perception of being alive and know well that life exists but that I am not part of it? ... managing such a painful ambiguity ... thus precipitating into a perilous spiral ... abandoning oneself to ... feeling lost because prey to a chasm that does not allow an escape ...

– ... a laborious search for a sacred act that can provide tranquillity and salvation?, interrupted David Mondine.

– The death of a mother is always a terrifying event ... feelings upset and disturbed, then ... frantically seeking a substitute figure ... who? ... a grandmother? ... a grandfather? The father was often absent as we've ascertained! ... courage consumed in a desire that crumbled with the passage of time ... remaining entangled in the mystery of his solitude ... who cannot understand such a state of mind? ... I have travelled to continents ... I went as far as Scotland to study ... was it a new way

64 *"I am a convalescent of the moment. / I live on the ground floor of thought / And watching life pass by bores me."*

to indoctrinate myself and to take care of my feelings? ... perhaps, at least I thought so ... I then began to travel the world setting sail from Glasgow for the Orient ... then fed up, after arriving at Marseille, I took the road for home ... travel without any benefit, certainly ... trying, in some way and laboriously, to lose my identity, my belonging to humanity, my monstrous will ... and Mário? ... Lisbon grasped him like a vice ... only Camarate, where his paternal grandfather lived, was a place that allowed him, still a boy, moments of healthy well-being ... he defined his horizon as the avenue of boxwood surrounding the house at Camarate so that nothing of what was beyond it could appear to him ... a claustrophobic existence ... the pleasure of being locked within a supportive world... awareness of an intimate and ferocious fear ... indeed nature could even appear treacherous ... like a rural vitality devoid of meaning and rich in illusions ... not wishing even to glance beyond the hedge which had to be an insurmountable barrier ... it is plausible therefore to state that, since then, death had forever marked an existence ... and my verses from *Opiário* are meant to recall these sentiments: *"Talvez nem mesmo encontre ao pé da morte / Um lugar que me abrigue do meu frio*[65]*"*... Agueda Maria Murinelo de Sá-Carneiro, his mother, died on the eleventh of December 1892 ... Mário was only two years old ... from then Mário became a widower child ... not being able to forget a lost love ... a great lost love ... what? ... no remembrance: not having any memory of the loved one ... a love destroyed before it became indissoluble ... an incestuous marriage marked by the premature death of the wife ... a dark death that violated the cathedral of happiness ... despising then what prevented the union with his great love ... hence the world appeared hopelessly hostile ... the mother-lover was ineluctably lost ...

Álvaro de Campos abruptly fell silent. He was moved. He began to slowly sip the wine. His stare lost in nothingness. Then she smiled sadly toward David Mondine. Nary a word. Intense

---

65 *"Perhaps not even next to death will I find / a place to shelter me from the cold I feel."*

looks. David Mondine also seemed spellbound by the sadness. Embarrassed, he began fiddling with the cutlery.

– And for you?, David Mondine suddenly asked, cleaving that awkward silence made of melancholy thoughts.

– Mário's life ran parallel to mine, replied Álvaro de Campos, reacquiring his bearing and clearing his voice. Another sip of wine to recover his lost composure. He adjusted his tie. He undid the buttons of his coat, revealing a burgundy silk waistcoat. He adjusted the monocle that seemed to want to desert the orbital cavity: – I do not believe in anything, he added: – I believe only in what my feelings attest as existing ... it's difficult to explain ... evolution? ... involution? ... no side taken ... like Mário, after all ... sight, hearing and touch ... seeing only through visual sensations ... hearing only through auditory sensations ... feeling only through tactile sensations ... I believe that Mário lost the possibility to take possession of his sensations when he forever lost the one who could teach him an appropriate use of those perceptions ... I insist, perhaps with reason ... and I want you to understood me ... if a person so beloved is taken from you, what remains but the despair of a life without hope? ... there ... being an orphan is heart-wrenching, but living with the ghost of a person you have lost causes an accentuated delirium, a brutal disequilibrium ... an alienation ... it is brutally lethal, infinitely lethal ...

– ... until an unrighteous choice ... until the disturbing intention to take his life?

– This is another matter ... we must know how to interpret it ... define in some way certain parameters ... do you understand what I'm saying? ... were you talking of suicide? ... himself mortally wounded ... there: mortally wounded ... murder of himself ... a sensible murder? ... perhaps nothing else ... I don't think that there's a substantial difference ... it is and remains a sensible murder because it is caused by an incontrovertible desire ... it is and remains a sort of exaltation of an instinct ... above all the unique necessity of a death due to a well-conscious act whose consequences are known ... dealing above all with an existential ambiguity ... but the real guilty party? ... that is the point: one who commits this sensible murder believes that he has the hopeful possibility of returning to his mother's womb ... it is and was essential to become the agent of the murder and, at the same time, the predestined victim ... no uncertainty ... having to be the protagonist as a single necessity ... killing to survive... the victim? ... he may not survive and, in this case, the act is truly unique since as executor he knows that he is also, and at the same time, a martyr ... an executioner-martyr and a martyr-executioner ... faced with that premise and with that ambiguous dilemma one is led to evaluate exclusively infinite possibilities so that one can avoid in some way the heart-wrenching suffering of the soul ... an ineluctably real aim ... and Mário? ... his childhood, as an orphan, was marked by mournful disequilibria ... *"E, por mais que procure até que adoeça, / á não encontro a mola pra adaptar-me*[66]*"*. What could be more true, in reference to Mário, than these verses from *Opiário*? ...

– Distressing solitude? Yet his family lived at Chiado ... an elegant district of Lisbon: so I am told ... yet it seems that it was already feeling the effects of a certain crisis of Portuguese society ... moving toward an institutional change ... small business seemed to stagger under the blows of an inevitable misery ... economic and social decline? ... many took to crossing the ocean ... to Brazil for example ... and others began to suffer from ineptitude and proven negligence ... public disorders became perilous habits ... but did the Sá-Carneiro family not suffer any discomfort or wrong? ... Mário's father, from what I've been told, enjoyed secure sinecures as a member of the army so that he could travel around half of Europe for free ... and his home was well run ... two servants and a nanny in his service ... assigned above all to the care of little Mário ... from where then did that distressing solitude and that emotional insecurity that you were talking about arise?

– I would say that Oedĭpus knows how to amuse himself among

66 *"And even if I search until I fall ill, / I cannot find a stimulus to adapt."*

the dark labyrinths of the deepest impulses … a mother, in fact … taking account of a mother whose parents had been, in some way, banned from right-thinking society, from the Sá-Carneiro family … there was that obscure story centred on a certain misappropriation of money … do you know that wretched story? … when this damned circumstance weighed on the mind of a child since the parents of his now-lost love, of his mother that is, had been ostracised because of an unfortunate event? … animosities not digested because perhaps they had never been digested by the mother? … an unjust and bitter legacy … perhaps the necessity to further defend his love … that story was, in my opinion, a terrible tangle of horrific acts of spite …

– … and what happened?

– Before Mário was born … misappropriation of funds to celebrate the promotion, from clerk to head clerk, of Mário's grandfather: José Leopoldo de Sousa Peres Murinelo … a party at *Tavares Rico*, a modern and elegant restaurant, taking réis from the Santa Casa da Misericórdia de Lisboa of which José Leopoldo de Sousa Peres Murinelo was an employee … also a political scandal since the Ministry, which oversaw the Casa, sought to cover up the story of the missing funds … corruption of the monarchical regime, someone said … Agueda Maria, Mário's mother, was also touched by the shame … no guilt: it's true … one doesn't choose one's parents … inevitable heartbreak even though Agueda Maria died of typhoid fever … the blame didn't fall on the children but on a father … what should not have happened did happen … Mário no longer wished to have dealings with his mother's family … a silence desired in order to protect a great love … and the despair for that great love? … a dark desire to cancel himself … to become lost in a tacit madness …

– And Oedĭpus?, David Mondine asked.

– Yes … what else but the insidious shadows of incest longed for but lacking … a compulsive desire fuelled by impossibility … a game of carnage to give rise to an endless lamentation … also to the conceivable search for a reason that was viable … this is the meaning of feeling a disturbing love for a mother …

it was necessary to sanctify Agueda Maria ... despise the whole Murinelo family ... to loathe his own father who, as a wandering dandy, had violated Agueda Maria, his mother, because she begat a son who would never be able to perform a supreme act of love ... was it then no longer necessary to consolidate his kinship in order to avoid interactions with strangers? ... why is love by a child always so boldly incestuous? ... Mário became lost in this sea of rash audacity ... would you like a dessert?, Álvaro de Campos suddenly asked as he poured the last drops of *Burmester* into his glass: – I mean some *pastéis de nata*[67]?

He ordered them without waiting for consent. In fact, he snapped his fingers and muttered something under his breath. A waiter nodded.

Silence while waiting. Looking around. Perplexity for what had been said. Thinking and rethinking. Mário and other things. Álvaro de Campos reflected on David Mondine as David Mondine reflected on Álvaro de Campos. Strange thoughts. Who actually were those two men sitting at a table in a restaurant in Aveiro? Perhaps two phantasms ready to discuss a man whom neither had ever met and known? At the moment also an odd interlude, since neither of the two interlocutors had the virtue of understanding who the one facing him was. A meeting determined by verbal and necessary ambiguity. A suicide, in fact! A heinous imprudence by that Fernando Pessoa who went about chasing the shadows that he himself had produced. Ambiguous shadows that might also have been a fiction born from a dark mind that seemed to conceal his innocuous folly in reworking his personality. Relying on that was difficult, indeed arduous. Dissociation? Some might have imagined creatures born ambiguously by rash dissociation. How to ask about that circumstance which seemed desired by Fernando Pessoa and by Angus Craston? Nothing else if not that Álvaro de Campos and David Mondine had to believe resolutely in that certain illusory world that had brought about their meeting. In fact they were there, in

67 Originally sweets made from puff pastry and custard with cinnamon.

Aveiro, in the attempt to discover the reasons for some unreasonable intentions regarding a death and, possibly even regarding themselves.

The waiter arrived while they were puzzling, with elusive archetypes, about why they were trying to understand what was necessary to understand about themselves. Living in a fictional world or creating a world in which it was possible to live even if one believed that that world was fictitious? Everything seemed to belong to a dream, like something that was generated by oneself.

Álvaro de Campos seemed to advocate this principle with an essential and convinced expression of certain reality. Also self-affirmation necessary to survive any ambiguity. It seemed fitting to complete the entrusted task even though there wasn't full awareness of the part that each one had to recite. Seeing, hearing, feeling?

Certainly Álvaro de Campos embraced the ethics of instinct and feeling since thought, as he preached with unusual conviction, was merely a disease. And David Mondine? Only a banal and ordinary investigator who necessarily had to adapt to propositions and to exchange views with a counterpart. In fact, Angus Craston had imposed binding terms.

– *A terra é semelhante e pequenina / E há só uma maneira de viver*[68]. Two verses from my *Opiário*, said Álvaro de Campos abruptly, while hastening to take a bite of a *pastél de nata.*

They sank their dessert spoons into that miscellany of corn, egg, cream and sugar. Small pastries, fragrant of oven and of lemon. An intoxication of the senses, which were heightened when a waiter, attentive to another sign by Álvaro de Campos, served two glasses of *Stüve*, a truly excellent '*porto*'.

They scooped the dessert greedily, rattling bowls wounded by the metal of the cutlery. They peered at each other from time to time without comment. Only nods of their heads to signal the pleasure in eating those *pastéis de nata.*

---

68 *"The world is small and the same everywhere / There is only one way of living."*

– A Bacchic orgy for free perceptions!, exclaimed Álvaro de Campos, clicking his tongue after savouring the dessert.

– I am sure that you would happily add: being both subject and object at the same time, David Mondine replied with an ironic touch, and added: – I must confess, with a certain reluctance and a certain intellectual carelessness, that you are a much more interesting man than Pessoa whom, however, I do not know in person ... you seem to be a person who conceals many fascinating personalities.

– Indeed I am subject and object at the same time ... it is sufficient to go about expressing my beliefs ... a man concerned only about himself and his feelings, one would say ... it is true after all ... it's my philosophy of life ... a way to participate in life very different from that of Mário ... Sá-Carneiro was sometimes an altruistic popinjay ... at times he was totally caught up in his claim "*os homens são eternas crianças*[69]"... at times he was engulfed in over-the-top sentiments so that he loved to attribute to others cruel and selfish omissions ... do you know his story in which he talks about his friend Raul Vilar? ... have you never heard of Raul Vilar?

David Mondine shook his head with negligence. Did it make sense to discuss the writings of Mário Sá-Carneiro to understand Mário's personality?

It's almost as if you had the opportunity to read his thoughts, Álvaro de Campos murmured in a low voice: – It is the story of a death by suicide.

They looked at each other in silence.

Then stereotyped smiles. Small sips to finish what was left of the port. Embarrassment, as well. Legitimate behaviours talking of real and presumed suicides. And Fernando Pessoa certainly knew Mário's story about his friend Raul Vilar.

– Also a story of reproaches, said Álvaro de Campos, above all of reproaches! ... Perhaps only those ... it would be good to talk about it ... to understand what it meant to Mário to write

69 Mário de Sá-Carneiro, Contos breves: "*men are eternal children*".

that story … 1910 … was he already compulsively thinking about death? … I don't know … it's certain instead that the search for death had to be an important step for him … that act and the person who performed that act must have remained in his memory … essential in my opinion … ineluctably essential … Raul Vilar had been forgotten, recalled Mário bitterly … that suicide had not been memorable … there: the banality of a suicide led inevitably to oblivion … keep that well in mind, my friend … a different way of being respected from mine … I am a decadent fool … I'm not and never will be important: I don't care to be … however I have in me all the dreams of the world … do you understand the meaning? … being in the moment in which I know I exist … nothing else then … I live because I know that I'm living, heightening my sensations … something else? … certainly all that which facilitates my being … singing what others believe to be foolishness while I experience it with sinful disquietude … listen… *"Minh'alma é doente. / Sentir a vida convalesce e estiola*[70]*"*… significant and explanatory verses from my poem *Opiário* … specify the meaning? … I have moved away from any altar of any conventional god … I have practised the exegesis of abnormality … I have sought to undoubtedly achieve an aware happiness … I can go about naked without shame … or perform other impulsive nonsense just to perceive sensations in complete freedom …

– … but is there something that you have in common with Mário? … with Mário's life? … with being Mário de Sá-Carneiro?, David Mondine asked, interrupting that logorrhoeic rant.

– it's difficult to explain … not for me, certainly … perhaps for what, for Mário, was the sense of appropriateness … how to say it? … insidious peculiarities … or rather impatient and harassing I would say, since … it was and is difficult to become aware of one's deepest intimacy … perhaps what united us, and it is my personal belief, was a particular sexuality … definitely … I'm not at all disturbed to tell you that, how to say it?, I go to bed with all

70 *"My soul is suffering / Feeling that life is improving but stifling."*

the sentiments ... hence I am a debauched panderer ... I am inevitably overwhelmed by all emotions so much so that I felt compelled to send, on the eleventh of June 1915, this salute to Walt Whitman: *"Grand pederast brushing up against the diversity of things / ... / You know that I am You and you are happy about this!"* ... do you understood what I mean?

– Perverse love?

– A latent perverse love ... have you forgotten what I mentioned at the beginning of our meeting? ... the object of his love had been taken away by death ... thus also his unjust desire? ... Mário perhaps ... had truly desired incest? ... then there was a murderer father ... it was certainly a thought that arose in the mind of the child Mário ... a father who did not want anyone else to be the lover of Maria Agueda ... impossible then to be like the father ... to be the father ... also to be the one who replaced the father ... what remained to him then? ... to identify with the mother ... to be the mother ... give in, necessarily, to the charm of men ... certainly not a debauched panderer ...

Suddenly he fell silent, staring into emptiness.

The room that welcomed Álvaro de Campos and David Mondine was now clear of patrons. Cleaned up, as well. Tables already set for the evening. Only one waiter remained, leaning against the doorway leading to the kitchens. He played with a napkin which he nervously rubbed with his hands. Bored, certainly. From time to time he glanced at that one table still occupied. Also at the two men who seemed intent on conducting a thoughtful dialogue. Appearances. Only obscure appearances upon a closer look. Perhaps phantasms. Duelling with meaningless words. Ambiguous reality. Suddenly it seemed that one of them was leaning forward as if asking for clarification. Then he leaned back awaiting answers. Faded figures. Suddenly the other, often adjusting his monocle, began to utter rigmaroles with calm courtesy.

The clock in the hall sounded three bells.

Awakening from the torpor of an insolent imagination. Closing time had passed long ago. A demanding job. Few réis earned. Being happy with that. Going back and forth with a few dishes of tripe and a bottle of wine. Obsessively at lunch and at dinner. Customers for the most part ungrateful. Small tips. Even slights. Some complaints. Watered-down wine. Someone denounced it. Asking for the house wine was always a gamble. The host-master knew how to take care of business. Unquestionably. Then those who lingered without taking into account the work of others. A very bad habit. The réis earned were very few. The snapping of fingers interrupted thoughts. There … the bill … yes, the Senhor in the coat.

The other man had already risen. A careful bow. A handshake. Establishing a friendship? Perhaps only conventional formalities. Then moving quickly toward the door. Certainly he had to cross the bridge and then wander off. The phantasms seemed to become lost in the unreal light of a town crouched along the banks of a lagoon.

VII

– Having agreed to meet you, it is as if I wished to consciously commit suicide, said Ricardo Reis, staring at David Mondine: – I could not refuse the peremptory and firm invitation made to me by Fernando Pessoa ... I am forever in his debt ... for my life, certainly ... for my poetry, perhaps ... an existence wilfully desired, sought, necessary ... it's difficult to explain ... undoubtedly we have travelled together in time and in the opportunities of a distinct and, at the same time, parallel life... and ever since that fateful meeting of the twenty-ninth of January 1912, toward 11 in the evening, when I revealed my literary inclination and the meaning of life, since Fernando was constructing his neo-classical theory, almost a scientific Neoclassicism accompanied by formal research ... everything seemed to unite us ... thus the conviction that it was not improper to be defeated when friendship and fame are no longer considered primary, essential values ... hence the conciliatory syncretism between Epicureanism and Stoicism ... hence the knowing thyself in an advanced and mystical process ... hence the compendium between formalism and awareness of the absurd ... it was because of those choices that I impulsively had the recondite desire to write, inspired by ancient lyric poetry ... to assimilate pagan worship, re-proposing it through writing ... to feel like an intrepid hero, with the truest feelings ... no practice of fundamentalist neo-paganism, let me be clear ... but the return to memory as a unique moment through that unusual melancholy that we Portuguese call *saudade* ... there is no possibility to delete from modern civilisation the magnetic, seductive, traditional influence of Christianity ... what was important was to propose myself, with judicious and sensible awareness, as a classical poet, as a follower of the esteemed Horace albeit going beyond his *Carpe Diem* ... why only "*Dùm loquimùr, fùgerit ìnvida / aètas: càrpe_dièm, quàm minimùm crèdula pòstero*[71]"?... counting myself then, in a specific manner, as a poet who pays tribute to antiquity as a perpetual salvation against any nefarious uniformity, against a peremptory lexicon and an old-fashioned idealism ... thus I began to versify with some irregular poems, drawn at random from my intimacy which already aspired to the celebration of pagan mythology ... therefore I began to sketch out very intimately and in a personal silence, aware of being able to be a narrator and poet ... hence I was stating that, alongside the specific peculiarities of different emotions, there was great structural simplicity and profound inspiring wisdom ... Fernando approved my predisposition, declaring that I was presenting myself to public attention as an esteemed epic poet of a classicism pervaded by a dark Epicureanism and a decadent paganism ... thus I owe him very much for teachings and wills ... I am repaying my debt by subjecting myself to what will certainly be inappropriate and surprising questioning ... yet it is only right to tell you that, at the moment, I have profound disagreements with Fernando ... literarily speaking ... different views on the life of the poet and in making poetry ... I conceive it without any linguistic interference and false propositions ... I long for a cultured, unique, ancient purity ... in a language that has the unmistakable marks of the Portuguese idiom ... but I am ready, on my part, to discuss this with my dear friend Fernando who, having spent his childhood in Natal, had his first literary experiences in English ... in another language, that is ... in an idiom that contrasts with our principal linguistic structures ... moreover there is also to discuss with my friend Fernando the need to oppose or not a certain prophetism, or rather the tendency to give specific attention to some utopian designs as if they were an

71 Horace I, 11: "*While we speak, envious time is flying away: / seize the day, and put little trust in tomorrow*".

irrepressible ideological necessity ... do you understand what I mean? ... I was and am a pure pagan ... I don't advocate absolute homogeneity and abhor any intromission of figures belonging to Christian Gnosticism ... a necessary separation ... however I'm hurt by the amicable dispute with Fernando ... I had much in common with him and I was bound to him by the same affection that binds Siamese twins ... our separation was, in fact, necessary ... just as was our following different paths ... because of a rash double-personality, no doubt ... because of split personalities ... because of different behavioural signs ... because of dark desires ... because of psychological processes ... because of dyslexic inclinations... because of mental industriousness ... because of dissimilar moralities ... because of a doctrinal corpus ... it is not permissible to save Christianity and at the same time play with esoteric doctrines ... oh, my God – he suddenly exclaimed: – it has been dawn for some time now ... it's getting late ... there is very little time I can dedicate to you ... I need to get away from this port ... maybe someone is squatting in a dark corner spying on me ... certainly some treacherous republicans ... you know? ... I come to the port every morning to watch the ships going overseas ... especially those sailing for Brazil ... a longed-for land: at least for me! ... there are many emigrants in search of fortune ... often mixed-use steamships: goods and people transported together ... the expatriates crowded in large dormitories in the hull ... receiving air only through the hatches ... they often contract diseases ... pellagra, malaria, scabies, which are extremely frequent ... they drink water stored in iron boxes covered in concrete ... they eat rancid and poorly preserved food ... all horrible things ... despite departing in search of a better life and to get away from this ungrateful country ... thus far about 28,000 peasants ... 20,000 without any trade ... 5,000 craftsmen and 200 labourers ... I would say that they will perhaps soon be joined by a poet ... it's necessary to stay in Brazil for at least 16 years to build a new life and a conscience ... and then, if desired, return home ... then perhaps, as payback, one could return with a stack of pounds sterling and profit unduly from a favourable exchange rate to accumulate a tidy sum of réis and spend them as one wishes... walking the streets of Lisbon again as a tourist and meeting phantasms lost in memory and to find them again in the dos Prazeres cemetery... returning home to savour Portuguese flavours ... going to Rossio to reach the restaurant *Irmão Undos* and enjoy a nice dish of boiled meat with a good glass of *Vinho do Tejo*... returning home to die in peace where *"o mar acaba e a terra principia*[72]"... thus I intend to reach Brazilian soil ... the country ruled by an *'old'* republic ... nothing to do with the Portuguese *sans-culottes*... here my feelings are well known and persecuted ... here a violent hatred of the lower classes is spreading... hence one can indulge in theft: considered a tolerable act, and not a crime ... here the atmosphere is imbued with strange revolutionary ideas under the despotic leadership of President Sidónio Bernardino Cardoso da Silva Pais... sooner or later someone will eliminate him, perhaps even some republican activist discontent with his authoritarianism ... in Brazil, instead, the monarchical aspirations are solid ... thus controlling any extremist outburst... adequate prerogatives are prefixed, with wise foresight and plausible speculatory reasons ... in agriculture, for example ... substantial allowances are offered to those who invest... the coffee and sugar plantations are attractive because they are very profitable... in Brazil my monarchical sentiments would be highly tolerated ... even appreciated ... therefore, I must decide to embark... to escape the boldness of this country... to set sail without too much talking...

–... tell me more about your life, interrupted David Mondine:– ... am I wrong or was your childhood marked by a healthy Jesuit education? ... and if I'm not mistaken, at least as far as I was told, you, despite ... how to say it ... being a university-educated doctor, have always rejected the profession ... you were and are, however, an accomplished Latinist and a valid Hellenist ... an expert in the Latin world and Horace in particular ... I was told about your authoritative and remarkable propensity for

72 José Saramago, *The Year of the Death of Ricardo Reis.*

sentiments ... correct? In memory of your profound knowledge, I am pleased to quote to you these verses:... *"Tù ne quaèsierìs* (scìre nefàs) *quèm mihi, / quèm tibi / fìnem dì dederìnt*[73]*"* ... because, in your opinion, leading an existence according to the rhythms of nature helps one to live without fears, without disquietude, in a sort of passivity ... acceptance of fate as an immutable event ... am I wrong perhaps? ... and then ... here I am perplexed that you cultivate a strong will to overcome any heart-wrenching melancholy through the existential philosophy of a Latinity that grants extreme freedom in governing one's life ... your Hellenism is pregnant with cultured refinement that seems to be inspired, in its erudite expression, by a certain Anglo-Saxon culture ... for me it is essential to understand some fragments of your life in order to compare it with that of Fernando Pessoa's other close friend ... Mário de Sá-Carneiro ... I would be very honoured to know if your life was ever crossed by troubled moments, by a melancholic Epicureanism ... I would be satisfied if I were to acquire further details of your contrasting and ambiguous friendship with Fernando Pessoa ... as far as I know, in truth from gossipy rumours, it seems that you are convinced that poetry is the representation of a concept transcribed by means of intense emotion whereas Fernando Pessoa is opposed to this assertion ... moreover, it seems that you do not at all believe, as Fernando does, that poetry can be the path leading to certain salvation ... I want to understand all this so as to be able, by applying an underlying transitive property, to untangle some knots in the life and death of Mário de Sá-Carneiro ... therefore?

– I will answer you with another short sentence from Horace's *Carpe Diem*, replied Ricardo Reis:– *"Ut melius quicquid erit pati*[74]*"*! ... meanwhile I can assure you that my life now takes place elsewhere, he added abruptly: – at least with the mind ... the disagreements are now past disagreements ... thus I have only faded

73 Horace, Carpe Diem: *"Ask not (it is forbidden to know) what fate the gods have assigned to me and to you."*

74 *"Far better to suffer what will happen."*

and blurred memories of some unpleasant disappointments ... what to say then? ... one thing is certain and I have no hesitation in expressing it with great regret but with certain affirmation ... my country has disappointed me ... deeply disappointed ... throwing itself, without a shred of historical consciousness, into the arms of a gang of disorderly republicans ... the fifth of October 1910 is for me a nefarious date ... it is the day of the proclamation of the republic ... a date to forget, possibly ... not to mention the obscene and tragic regicide that occurred earlier ... in Terreiro do Paço, here in Lisbon ... the king Dom Carlos and the prince-royal Dom Luis Filipe were assassinated ... the infante Dom Manuel was injured ... a massacre ... how is it possible to approve such heinous crimes by the republicans? ... and the republic then? ... it has not been able, in these years, to provide comforts to improve the condition of the Portuguese ... to add, moreover, the infamous decision to go to war without due knowledge or acceptable reasons ... aberrant stories ... not only this: it's true ... I think that true paganism con only be revived overseas ... certainly: far away from a home you love ... I am fanatically a classicist and I aspire to the purest classicism ... thus I hasten to exalt Homer's human existence ... do you understand what I mean? ... living according to nature ... without complaints and with satisfactory detachment ... literature is not an ecclesial expression ... one must understand this ... you have to forget about any intrusion ... free yourself from legacies imposed by force ... no mysticism or anything like that ... not to mention obscure metaphysics ... poetry is very much another thing ... it is not an ambiguous game that hides behind a conscious silence ... the ecclesial silence which ensures that nothing is as you would like it to be ... in short, using an idiom that is well calibrated and able to silence what may disconcert ... it is not at all necessary to engage in a devious manipulation of words if they have no meaning ... because, in short, everything remains in the mystery of a metaphysical language, in a subtle game of occult power. Therefore, serenity should govern life.

The wind was blowing insistently. Humid gusts, since

the slightly agitated sea caused the waves to break against the docks. Loving the sea. The Portuguese had loved it very much. Adventures of conquest. Travelling almost to the ends of the earth. Leaving the shadows of death to challenge the ships' wakes. They had also been cruel conquerors. Beginning at Calicut. 1502. Facing the Muslim fleet. Employing the 'line of battle'. Ships aligned bow to stern. Firing their batteries of cannons as 'broadsides'. Ships arranged 200 metres apart. The Portuguese Vasco da Gama ordered that the deaths be atrocious. Burning the Muslim ships with all aboard. Wealthy merchants with their families. Returning from a devotional journey to Mecca. A religion offended. Slaying the infidels. At the moment only silvery froths intertwined in a barely perceptible frenzy. The port was governed by an eerie silence. Brooding over one's melancholies. *Saudade.* Nostalgia of remembrance. A past never forgotten. Desire. Thus someone began to recall verses lost in his afflicted mind. Augusto de Carvalho Rodrigues dos Anjos. *Ao Luar. "Quando, à noite, o Infinito se levanta / a luz do luar, pelos caminhos quedos /minha tactil intensidade é tanta / que eu sinto a alma do Cosmos nos meus dedos!*[75]"

The horizons seemed to remedy sad disquietudes. The dawn appeared, like nightfall, with stirring colours. A pink, barely touched by a thin band of red, pierced a soft light blue that embraced the sky and plunged into a periwinkle sea. Also ships with lazily active stacks scratching the air with a dense, grey filament of smoke. The ships' powerful hulls were immobile, leaving a glimpse of the white band that barely ploughed the water. The busy chatter of sailors and travellers, ready to embark, imparted to the air an ambiguous and unreal rustling of voices. Also nostalgic and plaintive murmurs. Embraces and greetings. Leaving and being left. With emigration in their destiny. Hopes enclosed in obscure thoughts. The New World was a hospitable

75 *"When, at night, the Infinite rises/ in the light of the moon, in my gentle walking / my tactile intensity is so great / that I feel the spirit of the Cosmos in my fingers."*

land, it was said. Ancient land of an empire, but also a colony with a bastardised idiom.

Ricardo Reis looked insistently at David Mondine. They were sitting next to each other on two iron bollards. Reis was a short man, thin but with a vigorous appearance. A clean-shaven face. Shoes polished impeccably. A crumpled raincoat. A light breeze blew annoyingly. A floppy hat. An emblazoned walking stick.

– Why did you say that agreeing to meet me was like committing suicide? ... did you say it with conviction?, asked David Mondine, and he added: – a metaphorical suicide? ... or perhaps a suicide caused by fears? ... by disappointments? ... by an unusual anguish? ... or also by other causes? ... perhaps by depression? ... like Camilo Castelo Branco, I mean ... he was also Portuguese ... thus recalling unfortunate events ... especially for certain writers ... great exertions ... Camilo Castelo Branco, I repeat ... the author of over 250 works ... short stories, plays, novels ... do you understand why a painful event overwhelmed him? ... a writer, Camilo Castelo Branco, who committed suicide in the same year in which was born another writer: Mário de Sá-Carneiro, who perhaps committed suicide ... 1890 ... an unfortunate singularity? ... an occurrence that ineluctably offers reason to reflect ... thus I would like you to tell me whatever you can about Mário de Sá-Carneiro ...

– Undoubtedly Mário felt a seductive attraction to suicide ... as if it were a singular opportunity of life, replied Ricardo Reis with careful conviction: – What can I tell you? ... I barely knew Mário ... I followed, with some enthusiasm and particular criticism, his poetic, theatrical and narrative endeavours ... I could attribute to him some shortcomings, in literary terms ... I would say defects caused by an extreme desire to acknowledge instinctive impulses and profound emotions ... the incongruity of writing, then ... a singular tension able to combine a whole literary production into one ... to contain his spirit within certain absolute parameters ... to not stray from canons that specify a style, a way of saying, a preaching ... a certain originality, certainly! ... but above all a creativity that must define a work ... or better the set of works, giving it, it seems clear to me, a heterodox simplicity …

– … were you ever disappointed in Mário? … Mário often had the indelicacy to desecrate, as far as I've learned from malicious gossip, a cultural reality which drew on pre-established canons … was it then appropriate and necessary to appease what had been codified as literature? … his was a multifaceted poetry … so I've learned from light-hearted gossip … certainly the ego was and necessarily had to be the determinant fulcrum to narrate malaise and unease … I inferred, perhaps naively, a certain Manichean straining against an insecure and detested ego … a question of physicality? … of not accepting himself physically? … why then pour into his verses a deep frustration, as far as ignoring at times some syntactic rules? … thus, are the criticisms of some of his many detractors – who nonetheless acknowledged an exciting grandeur – exaggerated? … how can I provoke you in order to get from you a detached and exegetic judgement of Mário and his writings? … you were lovingly bound to Fernando Pessoa who was a close friend of Mário …

– I felt some regret because … yes because Mário had, and we do well to attribute this symptomatic attribute to him, the merit of great, rigid discipline … a discipline above all external … hence of consistency in the way of applying himself … of living his life … even in pain, in despair, in the perennial search for the existential meaning of life itself … something that was capable of satisfying him … do you understand what I'm trying to tell you? … take his death, for example … yes the death you are investigating … suicide or something else … it matters little at the moment … it is you who must solve this enigma … to satisfy Fernando … a death as an act that puts an end to your existence makes sense only if you are aware that, in that way, your destiny is determined … if you render yourself everlasting as the object of both bewilderment and interest … indeed it is so … it will be so … on the other hand, Mário certainly wished to thoroughly explore the sense of melancholy that afflicted him … have I been clear? … do you know in what circumstance and condition he was found dead in that hotel room? ... in Paris, I mean ... at the Hôtel de Nice ... there: great external rigour ... a melancholic and tragic discipline ... it's necessary to consider this element in order to understand Mário and the act that involved him ...

– ... existential obliquity? ... I am gathering opinions because it is necessary to understand completely what desire pushed Mário to perform such an act, which seemed to me, from information I've gathered but which is mainly irritating and disrespectful gossip, full of deliberate theatricality ... of consummate familiarity with dramatic sensationalism ... almost a dramatic turn of events that defined, in some way, his exacerbating ostentation wounded by a painful mental disorder ... a theatrical will which called onto himself, dead by means of a striking act, an attention which he had not seemed to have obtained up to then ... almost the desire to be the protagonist involved in collecting thunderous applause and maximal attention at the end of his show ... he was the star of the drama and could not be otherwise since the end of the play imposed the death of the protagonist.

– Instead, I recognised, in that probable act, his complex and neurasthenic spirit ... didn't you want to be informed of my opinions about Mário? ... here: I am giving you a clear example of his personality ... it doesn't matter if I ever met him or not ... I can talk about him as if I had frequented him assiduously ... knowledge through facts and events that involved him ... he was a man who never shared my beliefs ... perhaps for this reason I believe that I know him well even without having met him ... indeed I feel that I know him better than many other friends ... close friends ... friends of affairs, friends of delusions, friends of neurasthenias ... friends of Fernando, in short ... well then? ... in regard to what I'm telling you I can assure you, without fear of foolish denials, that Mário was undoubtedly a man of ancient temperament ... did I necessarily have to like him? ... perhaps because he added to his peculiar way of life, perhaps disordered, perhaps hysterical, perhaps even reckless, a visionary component, almost madly original, almost primitive ... I chose to frequent art on the sly in the same way that he decided to frequent it exuberantly ... as much as I am shy I can certainly state that Mário's sensational death fascinated me in a particular way ... we both slavishly sought or seek a path that could or can lead to death with as little pain as possible ... that it be in an Epicurean manner or by being overwhelmed by a heart-wrenching loneliness ... going on tiptoe or with a hue and cry ... certain of a full-blown mundanity ... one in one way, one in another ... but Mário's absolute and urgent need to appear after death so composed, so disciplined and ordered? ... what sense did he wish to give to his death? ... and to his life? ... it seemed to me that Mário wanted to amuse himself with a lethal game in the face of which he appeared indifferent, but to which he was bound for too long because he had witnessed, as a helpless boy, its cruel and atrocious occurrence, equally striking, equally excessive.

– Are you talking of the suicide of his friend Tomás Cabreira Júnior?

– January the ninth, 1911: a true watershed ... that day gave rise to a tragedy ... a tragedy that was supposed to be only amorous ... was it? ... that drama profoundly marked the life of the '*Bicho-cantante*[76]' as Mário de Sá-Carneiro was nicknamed by his classmates ... a death by suicide, then ... an event completely dissimilar to what Mário had always considered a loss of life ... I am borrowing the disconcerting and dark thought of Álvaro de Campos ... it is easy, according to Álvaro, to attribute the determination of Mário's suicidal act to the memory, never forgotten, of the loss of his beloved mother ... what sense did the death of Agueda Maria Murinelo de Sá-Carneiro have for Mário? ... perhaps it would be appropriate to believe that the memory of the loss of his mother had faded when dealing with a death different from that practised by Tomás Cabreira ... this is how Álvaro de Campos somehow expressed himself... have you had the opportunity to appreciate the man and poet Álvaro de Campos? ... an extraordinarily uninhibited man with his sexual and oedipal fixations ... an intentionally contradictory man ... a man

76 Singer of serenades.

passively engaged in the search for an ordered order that might concern a principal extravagance in behaviour ... it had to be wondered, therefore, if Mário de Sá-Carneiro had truly asked the question: why a death so strongly desired and so striking as that of Tomás Cabreira? ... I would say that Tomás Cabreira's suicide was a disturbing discovery for Mário ... a clearly shocking death ... nothing to do with dying in a cocoon-like place as had occurred for his mother Agueda Maria... windows ajar ... in her bed ... in her home ... the muffled sobs of bereaved relatives ... a sort of resignation marked by the signs of ritual mourning ... a well-attended funeral ... black clothes and garlands of flowers ... Álvaro de Campos would be very happy to gossip about such a mortuary organisation ... I am instead an individual who lives without cultivating any hope ... I abhor the disconsolate abandonment of oneself if one doesn't take care of the illusions of reality and the ambiguous reality of one's illusions ... Álvaro de Campos thinks in a completely different way ... certainly, sooner or later, he will become involved in artificial intrigues of hidden knowledge ... perhaps in cabalistic secrets ... meanwhile, there in the courtyard of the Camões school was a square full of rowdy boys who greeted Tomás Cabreira's striking and reckless act with astonishment and horror ... there died willingly a companion of writing and theatrical furores, at least for Mário de Sá-Carneiro ... also a fellow orphan ... Tomás shared with Mário the tragic melancholy for the loss of his mother at a young age ... commonality in a desperate disquietude ... the incestuous falling in love, Álvaro de Campos would have underlined once again and with reckless complacency ... falling in love that leaves an indelible mark, inexorably wounding ... a destructive fury that marks minds forever ... Tomás and Mário seemed to be linked by common destinies ... on that morning of January the ninth, the courtyard of the Camões school was packed, as I already mentioned, with pupils and teachers ... the gunshot rang out loudly ... a shot to the head ... blood and brain matter ... a horrid spectacle ... *"To a Suicide"* Mário later wrote recalling his friend's act ... it wasn't, in my opinion, an Epicurean and

Stoic act ... it was merely a fanciful act ... the need to show off amidst objective paraphrases and the hope of being an example ... almost an urgent need to show that one is *'eternal'* in death ... present and future ... hence one must never forget a writer who has committed suicide ...

– ... the not knowing how to lose: you mean? ... a clear rejection of what you, in some way, asserted as a solemn moment of a philosophical principle ... not being able to get used to the defeats of life by practising wise and balanced habits ... the not knowing how to bend, with reasonable awareness, to the Epicurean and Stoic doctrinal requirements ... the not being able to cede each intellectual and existential imbalance to a syncretic consciousness ... to an essential coagulation of a conscious pessimism ... therefore, paganism assigns to the Fates, daughters of the goddess of the night Nyx, indecipherable disorder and anonymous darkness, unfathomable and unimaginable futures ... and Mário?

– He sought asylum, flight from his homeland just as I seek it ... a hope? ... perhaps ... but, contrary to my spirit and to my desires, also the determined will to have a bit of Europe impressed in his mind ... a difficult endeavour ... forgetting first of all the teachings of pure classicism ... twisted provocations in language and form ... trusting himself to a word that had no meaning when compared to classicism ... thus losing the roots of our language ... neither Latinism nor Graecism ... no appropriate and restless sensibility in reconquering a glorious past ... have I perhaps expressed myself with too much arrogance? ... the academics certainly would have done so ... I owe much to Fernando and I would never dare deride a close friend ... I owe much to Fernando just as Álvaro de Campos owes much to him ... one must never forget gratitude ... life itself ... hence every time I look in the mirror – and I think the same happens to Álvaro – I have a feeling that sometimes Fernando is looking at me ... that often he approves and often he disapproves of my work ... it must be so if we have different personalities ... deliberately different ... but Fernando is always there to offer me suggestions that spring forth from his multi-faceted mind ... from a will that often overwhelms his being Fernando of *O Marinheiro* ... do you remember? ... a drama in which Pessoa summed up, openly confessing, all his paranoid obsessions ... who could ever have done so if not Fernando who, keeping intact his irony and his innate understanding of a complex and multi-faceted personality, went about sowing a miscellany of characters that were alive and with their own existence? ... not everyone ... especially not Mário de Sá-Carneiro who drowned instead, so they tell me, in a spiral of destructive melancholy ... did you ask me to tell you about Mário? ... there ... to me it seemed that he was a party to and involved in a choice of an irritating literary mish-mash which, I believe, can be called *Literatura de Manicomio*, as Mário himself wrote in an article of 1915.

– A real madness that the imagination might have saved? ... I believe that, in regard to what you have said, a so unstable life and a death so unfortunate, like those of Mário, were due mainly to the lack of a thaumaturgical imagination ... to not wishing to yield to a controlled madness ... imitating Fernando ... exiting from a narrow self to live in parallel worlds ... in a mirror of his longings ... in a trusted mirror... in a mirror desired with determination ... and, on the occasion, to also digest his anxieties, accompanied by ignoble but healthy drinking bouts ... Mário precipitated instead, as far as I am able to understand, into painful insecurities for having dodged, for his own reasons and sad emotional insubordinations, the Orphic initiation ... he was denied a teaching, moral or immoral as you wish, able to contemplate the presence of the human and the divine in being ... trying to live after the birth and publication of the first issue of the magazine *Orpheu*? ... wasn't it then that he proposed to defend a profound and different concept of existence? ... wasn't it then that he decided to explore the unfathomable meaning of life?

– Thus enclosing the uneases of living in insufferable intellectual contexts? ... that is perhaps the reason for the need to leave his homeland and to go ... go, go ... why look elsewhere for counterpoints of suitable intellectualisms? ... certainly not because he was attracted by something that cannot be experienced here, in Portugal ... I am very intrigued by being able to cross the ocean and find myself in Brazil ... in a stubbornly desired exile ... forging a new life there ... far away from a treacherous and corrupt republic which now governs my country ... it never entered Mário's mind to abandon his homeland as a political choice ... republic or monarchy was the same thing for Mário... he hated his country because it was full of a bourgeois gang in slippers and dressing gowns ... of towns all the same in a rhythm of obsessively immutable life ... of irritating *azulejos* that defined an archaic model of life ... of the cadence of a spoken language that the bourgeoisie and the common people had deformed ... of all that which, after all, was Portuguese ... which was provincial ... which was trivial ... perhaps Mário wanted to be a missionary of diversity and of an incisive artificiality ... he wanted to be unique ... the exile who had chosen exile as a moment of rebirth ... what happened instead? ... well: finding himself alone in a city that was apparently so full of life and eclecticism as Paris ... a choice made in a manner which, in some way, might offer the license for diversity ... do you understand, my friend? ... a diversity that Mário thought would mean above all ... being someone ... but he lost himself in desperation ... Paris welcomed him as a derelict ... even amidst the last lights of the last years of the *'belle époque'* ... even amidst a triumphant bourgeoisie that was deceiving itself ... with a tragedy at the gates ... the great war which was now a voracious beast ... was Mário aware of it? ... everything now appeared decrepit despite hopeful signs ... only madness seemed to govern a world that no longer wished to be the same ... decadence was a vigil prophet ... concealed pains seemed to be hidden in the latest flashes of false prosperity ... Mário was trying to revive, at least in his writings, what could no longer exist ... longed-for but disappeared beauties ... extinguished vitalities ... desired disinterests now swallowed up by dark but compelling necessities ... God, a war that was approaching rapidly! ... in desperate nostalgia for a time now past, Mário seemed to want to persistently follow his own path ... to distinguish himself in order to exist in an absurd intemperance that certified a vulgar decadence ... excellent writings: it's true! ... fascinating writing exactly because, in my opinion, dictated by a mind corrupted by a melancholic depression that gave him no respite ... hard to make peace with himself when he did not want peace ... the psychic unease was now preponderant ... and the fantastic worlds he had yearned for? ... history took another course ... exile was not profitable ... perhaps it would have been necessary to cross some ocean and find himself among people who spoke an idiom very similar to ours ... Paris was turning off its lights ... useless to frequent cafés, boulevards, unknown intellectuals, indigent artists, mediocre painters, poor devils penniless and jobless and to then discover that reality and ideal could never belong to him because they were merely the result of a mental dissociation ... a mental dissociation, repeated Ricardo Reis forcefully.

By now he had abandoned his bollard. He walked restlessly peering at the harbour. Indecent debris floated all about. Peels of fruits. Leftover vegetables. Large oil slicks and rat carcasses. A city that seemed to become lost in an unnatural humiliation, in a desired neglect, in a reprehensible abandonment.

Suddenly Ricardo Reis stopped and looked at David Mondine insistently. His eyes were moist. Barely perceptible tears. Then he raised the collar of his raincoat and quickly walked away.

VIII

– A certain Fernando Pessoa, who, I am told, is a poet of some renown but whom I do not know or do not remember having known, has advised me in a short letter, with vague words and very questionable accents, to speak with you, albeit without having given me reasons and principles of such an arrogant imposition, which I believe is the result of modern practices never accepted by those who, like me, live in a classical world that abhors violence of sayings and thoughts, said a man dressed in a broad tunic that seemed to be in a Roman style almost as if he were *rerum dominus.*

The head was with tousled white hair in disarray, and the chin with a long and bushy white beard, framing a face with a wisely penetrating but rashly restless look. He was a tall man and strangely altered in his ways and words. Iniquitously mad.

It was not clear if he was consciously pleased or bravely disappointed. A moment earlier, he had ended a frenzy of verses and reminiscences which seemed suddenly drawn from distant memories, from thorough studies or from arbitrary wills. Especially from Greek. A *koinè diàlektos* or common language capable of overcoming any dialectal particularity. A cultured language, in short. Rigorous cadence. Extraordinary overviews. An emphatic lexicon. Original metaphors. Perhaps Aeschylus. Perhaps *Prometheus Bound.* Certainly Aeschylus. Undoubtedly *Prometheus Bound.*

Suggestions or something else?

David Mondine had been hopelessly sequestered by a personality, by a character, by a role ... someone had then murmured:

– cognitive hysteria ... deliberately improper acts ... not being able to act otherwise ... laboriously seeking a way of being ... lying to others so as to be able to lie to himself ... an infamous game to be interpreted at any cost ... thus confirming his existence ... truly an ugly story ... psychic alterity.

The warnings that David Mondine had received were eloquent. Hysterical paranoia or paranoid hysteria ... an equivocal concatenation ... wandering with lamentations ... expressing himself with delusional certainties ... oxymorons of lively madness ... versifying because it is a liberating act ... presaging, with astute determination, foreboding divinations ... studied delirium ... contemplative and satisfied alienation ... crazy escapades ... retreating into a world to escape from every inauspicious decadence ... the contemporary world, then.

The warnings had been clear. David Mondine was keeping them in mind.

The name of that cultured and mad reciter was Dr António Mora, a graduate in law, at least according to what had been written in the guest register at the time of admission, and he was exactly, so it appeared, the man whom David Mondine wished to meet in order to exchange words and deepen his knowledge of Mário de Sá-Carneiro.

He appeared mad, but only to those who were not used to living in the time in which Dr António Mora intended to live. For him, it was much better to live as an odd sort, intending to experience a time in which it was possible to affirm wills very inflexible toward any vulgar modernity rather than to live as a sane man accustomed to attitudes that did not suit him. What was truer than a false truth?

In that sanatorium to which he had been confined, his habit of babbling his profound revulsion for all that was modern was well known for some time. Looking back to ancient times, to the rule of the gods when the magnificence of thought was determined by philosophical wisdom. Then, with thought that became philosophy, civilisation as such made sense. No intrusion into shameless manias generated by Christian education which did not allow abstraction from morality and from the practice of good governance. There was, moreover, to recall what had been reported, that the modernist educational concept harboured strong selfishness, a humanity judged only by a rampant Christist faith, determination of interdependence between that kind of selfishness and a type of second-rate humanity.

Above all, that doctor did not seem to remember much of himself or of the reasons why he was confined in that *asilum*. Indeed, he was not interested in knowing such reasons because he was now isolated in a docile paranoia and in an improper and ordered hysteria.

He was confined in that *asilum*, so it was said, by a deliberate action of certain relatives, rather alarmed by his dangerous persecution mania. Also on account of insidious, albeit satisfying, identifications. Being himself, despite being another. Also for a toga that he now wore. Also for his mind so inclined to be what he might be living in another time.

Was amusing himself with Aeschylus and his *Prometheus* a determined way to find himself? An inappropriate or falsely appropriate choice? A sort of rebellious titan. A tragic but free hero. A will inflexible toward any unconscious deviation. Resolute, determined consciousness. An ideal to imitate. A reserved spirit against the infamies of the new. The consolidated resources of the past had been lost. Unpropitious acquisitions were the patrimonies of the present. Vulgar modernism. The present was a consolidated decadence caused by improper and deceptive convenience. Civilisation corrupted by compromise of the spirit. Iniquitous degeneration.

Often, after listening to devious insinuations and hostile gossip by relatives, António Mora had been overwhelmed by a strong psychoneurosis marked by delirious, but not at all insidious, symptoms, concerning only that modernity which, for some but certainly not for him, was a distinctive sign of universal progress.

Sociological mania, if you wish, which repudiated the hypocritical lesson of Christianity to be inflamed instead in praise of the sacredness of ancient Greece. A wise doctrine, in itself objective because it did not consider necessities as primary elements. Nothing could be simpler. The doctrinal principle was to follow the course of nature. Thus explaining, without fear of contradiction, the dutiful need to accept the dialogue and not the opposition between consciousness and matter.

António Mora, as had been established by clinical confidences obtained in that pleasant sanatorium, practised with absolute prerogative a convinced battle against *Christism*, the single cause, in his view, of the world's decline. Since the term *Christism* was repeated endlessly by António Mora, there was the necessity, perhaps through ignorance or perhaps through obtuseness, to know what, indeed, it was. There were many hasty interpretations. Many general indications. Many syntactic explanations, nonetheless without ever providing comprehensible specifications.

Hence there were many glosses drawn from etymological terms amidst incomprehensible lemmas, obtuse periphrases and vulgar circumlocutions, until a certain Dr Gama Nobre, who, it is said, closely resembled António Mora, provided a methodological explanation that drew on his theological studies in his youth.

Dr Gama Nobre explained, among fleeting memories and a few conscientious testimonies, what was *Christism*[77], at least in the belief of the followers of paganism. He specified that it was a sort of frustrating determination in creating occult groups able to spread the Christian faith throughout the world. A true hegemonic and tyrannical tendency. A well-determined political premise. The rash firmness of will, in short, to lead part of humanity. Certainly the weakest and most gullible part. Leading it by the hand toward an inevitable decline. Thus acting, with careful and compelling warnings, against mysticism and a secret and despotic subjectivity.

77 According to Pessoa, Christism was an autonomous religion, a pure paganism, a sort of syncretism.

David Mondine became aware of these mystical–philosophical prerogatives of António Mora after affiliating to his investigation, with persuasive words and dignified dissertations, various people living in that sanatorium. Insidious speculation if there was the possibility of being led astray by such manifold thoughts, if one allowed one's mind to conceive as possible truth what *Christism* was affirming.

Meanwhile, António Mora, with his proven aversion to *Christism* and its apostles, went freely about reciting memorable verses imbued with distressing laments and ancient memories. There had occurred, in fact, what necessarily must have occurred since others persevered with impunity in arrogating to consciousness, and thus to their faith, the certainty that reality existed precisely since it was dictated by faith...

"Look upon me, what treatment I, a god, am enduring at the hand of the gods! Behold with what indignities mangled I shall have to wrestle through time of years innumerable.[78]*"*, repeated a voice in harmonious accents. It was affirming and supporting different thoughts. Many and different, then. Those verses seemed to want to evoke consciences not yet lost in the insanity of modern religiosity. Thus it was licit, indeed dutiful, that everyone could and should see in each object something different from what that object was. Only remembrance and memory defined what was that object. Thinking and discussing about what one thought. An extravagant occupation that seemed to be expressed with unreasonable and unhealthy intransigence.

That sanatorium, in which Dr António Mora was forced to stay, was very famous for alleviating the sufferings of miscreants or for treating alienated oddballs. It was located in Cascais. In Cascais, it is true, where everything seemed of another sort and merit. A renowned and very salubrious place for beneficial rest and thoughtless revelry. Where, it was said, the land ended and the sea began. The climate and ocean offered warmth, grandeur, a lush tropical vegetation. Shady avenues, quiet streets

78 Aeschylus, *Prometheus Bound.*

and sensual whorls of wind. A place where neglect and negligence were avoided. Well protected by the imposing bulk of the *Cidadela* fortress. A strip of land called the *'Portuguese Riviera'* where Lisbon's wealthy bourgeoisie preferred to pass the hot summers and temperate winters. Hence the negligence in showing itself indifferent to whether the country was ruled by a monarchy or a republic was intoxicating. One was compelled to listen, certainly reluctantly, to *A Portuguesa*[79] instead of *O Hino da Carta*[80]. And to recite "*Saudai o Sol que desponta / Sobre um ridente porvir; / Seja o eco de uma afronta / O sinal do ressurgir*[81]" instead of "*Viva, viva, viva ó Rei / Viva a Santa Religião / Vivam Lusos valorosos / A feliz Constituição/ A feliz Constituição*[82]". One was even forced to accept the right to strike. However, it was permissible to retaliate against the insolence and arrogance of workers by applying a lock-out. One could also be content that, spending time in Cascais, one had the chance to live side by side with a rich, snobbish English community that had taken possession of that strip of land because it loved to spend the winter in a warm place, and for just a few pounds. Indeed, one could stay there for 25 days for just 15 or 17 pounds, including the cost of the round trip.

Hence the Lusitanian community living there had the benefit of being able to assimilate English customs and manners that seemed very suitable to those whose aim in life was to acquire affectation and refined tics. Thus faces burnt by the sun and smiles open to compromises were encouraged. Also skin creased by the years, but shiny with oil.

– My name is David Mondine, said the investigator slightly tilting his head toward António Mora. He held him back by lightly touching the man's arm when he began to stroll once again among the vegetation of the garden. He was also reciting

79 National anthem of the Portuguese republic.

80 National anthem of the Portuguese monarchy.

81 *"Salute the Sun that rises / Over a gleeful future; / Let the echo of an offense / Be the sign for a comeback."*

82 *"Hail, hail, hail oh King / On our holy religion rest / Lusitanians fired with valour / Hail our blessed constitution / Hail our blessed constitution."*

verses accompanied by marked gestures. *"Such then as this is the vengeance that I endure for my trespasses, being riveted in fetter beneath the naked sky*[83]*"*, he murmured, very pleased.

An impulsive gesture that of Mondine, but not aggressive, so that he could promptly add while chasing the briskly moving man: – I'm the friend of that Pessoa who has supported my cause ... I asked to meet you ... some miserable questions without bothering you too much ... I have an urgent need ... the desire for adequate knowledge ... nothing scandalous or indecent ... nothing that would distract you from your balanced poetry ...

– ... and are you, my friend or unconscious enemy, a senseless modernist as it is customary to be today?, Mora asked, peering at Mondine with worried attention.

He then abruptly halted, stared at him for a moment and added, versifying: – *"Look upon me, what treatment I, a god, am enduring at the hand of the gods!*[83]*"*, after which he quietened and then resumed with sordid irony: – have you vices? ... have you evident or concealed defects? ... Are you perhaps a person who does not like Aeschylus and his *Prometheus*? ... Who repudiates classical antiquity? Who does not defend classical civilisation because he does not see it for what it truly is: a beacon of all progress? ... this house for madmen could, nonetheless, welcome you with satisfied determination ... indeed there are infinite possibilities to survive as best possible ... leading your life in the world and in the way that you wish without minding unfortunate treatments and heinous considerations of false friends or horrible relatives ... the sacrifices are very modest ... being at peace with yourselves and letting others know that you are afflicted by obscure desires, by incurable imbalances ... being considered mad: it is enough ... nothing more ... compared with a dark, tumultuous modernism ... mass killings due to egocentric desires ... imitating models of devious gang leaders ... dictates from a single school of thought ... philosophy approved by young charlatans ... exacerbating selfishness ... lives forced into singular practices ...

83 Aeschylus, *Prometheus Bound.*

defending one's own backyard ... false and vulgar humanitarianism... Christianity, then! ... sell yourself to the highest bidder?... Psalm 26, 27?... "*The Lord is my light and my salvation; whom shall I fear?*"... or: "*Requiem aeternam dona eis Domine?*"... thus complacently accepting superfluous testaments to peace and faith?... "*Look upon me, what treatment I, a god, am enduring at the hand of the gods*[83]!", he continued to recite and added – thus I free myself from insulting and persecutory bothers ... I return to a pagan Stoicism ... I regret a loss ... of an ancient life ...

– Mário de Sá-Carneiro ... I'm here to acquire information about this poet ... do you have memories of this Mário de Sá-Carneiro? ... I ask you to have reflective patience ... perhaps you can give me your past impressions if and when you met Sá-Carneiro ... if you met him ... certainly: he was a modernist poet, perhaps horribly modernist for you ... a reductive exemplification: it's true ... I'm trying to become accustomed, in some way, to your judgemental categories ... I well understand, after listening to what some people have told me about you, that you are only interested in wishing to accustom yourself, with obstinacy and ineluctably, to the truth, to metaphysics and to the practice of paganism, but about Mário ... about Mário then ... his death, his supposed suicide should induce you, for fleeting moments, to put aside your strong principles ... a death, a presumed suicide: I say and I recount ... and you? ...

– A death, a suicide?, António Mora abruptly asked and stared intensely at David Mondine: – a death ?, he wondered again and then began reciting to himself: – Oh, death, "*death, which would be the end of all suffering*[83]"... Mário de Sá-Carneiro?... I remember, perhaps ... in fact ... if I'm not mistaken it was a certain Dr Gomes who told me about it ... a slothful psychiatrist who frequents this place of infamy and of delight without shame or praise ... perhaps Dr Gomes told me that ... why did he not announce to me the death of that Sá-Carneiro? ... never knew, I believe! ... perhaps I had an equivocal and provocative message from Pessoa? ... it's very strange, but this Pessoa continually intersects my life ... maybe he's only a shadow ... maybe just a ghost ... I seem to perceive him also in all his physicality ... madness allows any oddity ... certainly I feel a strange and fascinating bond ... I can't explain it with appropriate words ... sensations, only perceptual sensations for which ... yes, I feel that I was, in a certain sense and for what is called a transitive property, in contact with that Mário you were talking about ... true? ... it was surely so! ... Dr Gomes ... perhaps because ... yes ... perhaps because ... now I seem to remember ... let us talk about this Mário who took his own life ... am I wrong perhaps?

– Presumed suicide, I would say ... I was instructed to determine whether ... it was Pessoa who proposed a thorough investigation of what happened ... what did Dr Gomes tell you? ... and why did he bother to report to you on what happened? ... are you interested in suicide or in the way one commits suicide? ... death as the end of all suffering?

– Paganism offers clever customs already experienced in antiquity ... wills unyielding to any mish-mash of false fideism ... there ... death as misfortune or bad luck? ... determining with the senses, nothing else ... confirmed knowledge ... knowing means confirming with one's senses ... distrusting rash theological comforts ... do you consider it unbecoming if I affirm that Christianity has been, at the same time, opium and cocaine of modern European peoples[84]?... the path to the truth is often full of mental ambushes if you don't wish to trust true and pure Stoicism ... only positive and, I would say, objective propositions... becoming lost? ... it's easy to be imbued with resignation because we are promised gratification, rather an excellent reward ... a quite scurrilous thing ... are you afraid of death? ... this Mário de Sá-Carneiro wasn't: I suppose ... a modernist artist? ... Strength would have spoken thusly to Prometheus: *"Can mortal men ever alleviate your agonies? By no true title do the gods call you Prometheus; for you have need of a Prometheus, by means of which you will escape this fate[83]"* ... do you understand what I mean? ... Christianity has deprived man of all thought,

84 António Mora, *Obras.*

suffering and philosophical reflection ... an unfortunate thing ... And Mário de Sá-Carneiro? ... I didn't know him, but ... that Dr Gomes told me a lot about him ... I seem to have known him also because of Pessoa ... why: you will ask? ... perhaps to arouse my consciousness as a madman *sui generis* ... were you asking me about suicide even while not knowing for sure if that suicide actually happened? ... doubts ... only doubts ... and Senhor Pessoa? ... unconscious embarrassments since Senhor Pessoa took very little interest in my fate, even though ... even though wishing to keep alive an unusual confidence ... an unbreakable bond also in madness ... whose madness? ... a strange thing, in truth ... it seemed as if obscure and bizarre bonds united us but here ... I believe that it was mainly he who desired that I be confined in this sanatorium ... I don't know the reasons or the considerations ... reasons of clearly established and not clearly established insanity? ... it's possible ... one always avoids dangers if one doesn't wish to look back with conscious and lucid necessity ... referring to the enviable ancient world ... do you understand? ... sometimes we hide under various personalities in order to avoid dangers but without knowing how to take the right path ... it's easy to have available various ways of life and to languish in existential diversities ... to be this and not to be it ... someone is trying ... but without wisdom ... with wisdom I have embraced a single precept ... I am, or at least many believe so, a madman ... in fact I don't respect demonstrated beliefs in order to relieve myself of the suffering of an essential ambiguity ... being without entirely being ... or being by being many ...

– ... but death? ... Mário de Sá-Carneiro's death? ... what can you tell me about what Dr Gomes referred to you when he told you of the death of Mário Sá-Carneiro? ...

– ... an obscure discussion, in truth ... even though I have a great ability to understand what others do not understand because I am interested in comprehending languages and unusual behaviours ... crazy ones as well ... even ones that are ancient in conduct and in beliefs ... and yet I was unable to interpret the meaning of the cryptic message that Senhor Pessoa sent to me by means of that ambiguous person who is Dr Gomes ... also this seemed to me an unscrupulous pact between madmen ... there was to verify personalities and characters ... who indeed was Dr Gomes and who Pessoa? ... odd identities ... identities ... only in the face of such an inexplicable mish-mash of identities was it possible to understand the reason for the firm desire to tell me, through suitable words and a certain devious discretion, that a certain Álvaro de Campos and Ricardo Reis had also been informed ... I have never had the honour of knowing these men even though, as Dr Gomes reported to me, they had with me, as with Senhor Pessoa, certain affinities ... affinities of gender? ... of thought? ... of life? ... I asked with argumentative timeliness ... perhaps, as I was led to suppose, affinity of dissertations ... or also of origins ... but which ones? ... it is difficult to characterise this last word which means a lot just as it means very little ... origin then? ... but of beginning or of commencement? ... distinctive mark of an initial act or an ontological trait or of being as such? ... is the question I posed too clever? ... I don't think so: it was only the search for an appropriate terminological use to specifically indicate a meaning ... in response to that request for clarification Dr Gomes seemed disoriented, as if afraid to show far more than he had the possibility of saying, or confessing, or even revealing ... a death, he added then, in a faint voice almost as if afraid to say what he was about to say and, mumbling his words, that it seemed perhaps a suicide ... even if appearance can sometimes be deceiving ... he continued then repeating the name of the dead man clearly ... Mário de Sá-Carneiro the poet, he said ... I wondered then who he was if Senhor Pessoa had taken the trouble to inform me so quickly ... a legitimate and not a loaded question ... should I have known this Mário de Sá-Carneiro?, I asked insistently ... Dr Gomes's reply seemed very difficult to comprehend, perhaps because of the psychic alteration that often overwhelms me ... it was not a clear and transparent response since he replied that this Mário, possibly a suicide victim, had been caught by death without Senhor Pessoa having interacted in the slightest with dates and lives because he was not, let us say, a heteronymous figure ... from the Greek ἑτερωνυμία, that is ... from *héteros* as other and from *onoma* as name ... instead Mário Sá-Carneiro, Dr Gomes told me with resolute authority, was very different from me who gave myself airs with unconscious desire and false laziness, with a madness that could well have been a false madness decreed only by one who wished to engage precisely in madness so as not to show to the world his own mad delirium made of ... for example: of depersonalisation, of alcohol-induced ravings, of phobias, of social anxieties ... just as, one might have thought, for Álvaro de Campos and Ricardo Reis who, beyond personal and identity conflicts with Senhor Pessoa, had to digest arrogant vendettas if Mário de Sá-Carneiro had ever been of a mind to meet them, to exchange thoughts or dialectics with them, to recognise the meaning of life conceived so differently, almost as if they conducted a falsified and mistaken existence while Mário was almost proud of the accomplished fullness of his ... I believed, at that point, that Dr Gomes was afflicted with an unexpected attack of paranoia since his words were entirely devoid of a correct meaning just as they were not credited with appropriate wisdom ...

– And Mário de Sá-Carneiro?

– Of Mário de Sá-Carneiro I only have information gained, as I mentioned to you, from that incongruous messenger who was, so it seemed to me, Dr Gomes ... I had many doubts about his real function as an agent ... was he a fictitious or real agent? ... hard to say ... some inmates comforted me reporting that this Gomes had already been seen wandering in this sanatorium in the company of a man who had come here for his own interests, which seemed to be purely literary interests ... there was talk of the necessity to collect sensations for a narrative that was to be entitled *Na Casa de Saúde de Cascais*[85] ... returning to what Dr Gomes told me, it seemed to me that his words had been drawn out with a certain melancholic reluctance ... indeed, he emphasised: don't be alarmed! ... that there was only a certain importance, according

85 *In the Cascais Sanatorium*: written by Fernando Pessoa between 1907 and 1910.

to Senhor Pessoa, that I knew of Mário de Sá-Carneiro's death because Mário was a scandalous irregular like me ... just like me ... in fact he had not managed to control his self-destructive instincts, thus going about in an apparently fictitious world just as I retired to this place wishing to live in a likewise fictitious world ... I was quite shocked ... what did he mean in truth? ... that it was a madness desired to dominate my life and that of Mário? ... or perhaps ... what?

– It seems that your paganism fully satisfies you ... I understand the choice... if I'm not mistaken it seems to be a strongly considered philosophical necessity ... was yours a conscious diversity? ... perhaps Senhor Pessoa had to pursue different experiences ... perhaps he came here in disguise, in the company of Dr Gomes, to understand if his choice was appropriate and how it was possible to live with it rather than take notes for a possible bizarre story ... a necessity perhaps to contemplate the possibility of living different lives ... choices perhaps to make with cautious certainty ... or which he had already made but that he was troubled and fearful in revealing to you how it was an ambiguous and disordered decision ... do you understand? ... a sadly subtle and precarious game ... different personalities no longer able to be controlled ... to be defined in their existential context ... Mário meanwhile ... Mário ready to demonstrate a path ... a mad choice to reaffirm an innate madness ... as if also Senhor Pessoa had been afflicted with a madness able perhaps to contain Mário's innate madness, freeing propositions alternative to suicide ... perhaps Senhor Pessoa wished, in truth, to know to what extent, well beyond the chronic alcoholism that could lead to death from cirrhosis, it would be possible to live without plunging into the unconsciousness of a chilling madness ... perhaps he thought that this was possible through specular references or choosing a painful truth, like a probable and striking suicide, able to give once again meaning to his dignity as a mad and desperate man ...

– ... dignity of life? ... it's likely ... what can I say? ... I've thought long and hard about my existence and the pagan world in which I have consciously taken refuge ... I've reflected on some of Dr Gomes's words concerning Mário de Sá-Carneiro and the last years of his life ... strange reports often confused by a desire to compare gestures and acts of that Mário with my life ... I cannot tell you if there was some truth in what Dr Gomes said with a certain malice ... undoubtedly some events in the life of Mário de Sá-Carneiro struck me on account of a certain consonance with my choices ... suggestions? perhaps ... I can't deny it ... undoubtedly a mental instability rendered me Mário's companion in misadventure ... similar observations in countering the ambiguous game of life ... also the search for something that escaped us ... the uncontrolled desire for immortality ... whether it was madness or death ...

– ... madness or death? ... death and madness?

– one begins, in fact, to amuse oneself in a lie ... perhaps with petty regularity or petty will ... let us recall what people often think: that madness is nothing but a principal ineptness in controlling our feelings ... true? ... wished or desired irrationality? ... also the subtle charm of a world that has become lost in memory and which one seeks to recover by living it, or that one has not been able to fix in memory ... Senhor Pessoa, meanwhile, should well know something about it according to the ramblings of Dr Gomes ... it seems that he often thinks, and sometimes with sincere regret, of Mário now that he is dead ... regrets, certainly ... also afflictions ... desperate letters, Dr Gomes told me, in the last days of Mário's life ... exchanges of letters to declare themselves similar in existential anguish ... in some way all was predictable at least for someone, like me, who lives life following Prometheus ... yes Prometheus the titan ... Prometheus the thief ... Prometheus whose *"Godlike crime was to be kind, / To render with thy precepts less / The sum of human wretchedness*[86]*"* ... certainly an imprimatur ... amidst signs and meanings ... a premonition ... a wise premonition if you extort the gods ... Prometheus's wisdom is sometimes considered stupidity, like his false

86 George Byron, *Prometheus.*

knowledge ... thus I feel similar to him who propagates a truth that the false gods do not wish to be propagated ... Christianity certainly ... a clear sign of overt madness? ... a toga is a suitable garment to support a madness which is often appropriate and beneficial for all those who proclaim themselves new gods ... thus also in aspiring to a death which is restless madness ... a suicide desired and procured or also acute alcoholism to satisfy basic desires ... in 1913 Mário confessed publicly, Dr Gomes told me ... a story: *The Confession of Lucio,* while ... while Pessoa wrote the verses *"All my hours are made of black jasper / all my anxieties are carved on a marble that does not exist"* compiling *Hora Absurda* ... thus shattering hopes as long as they were not extreme ... testimonies of loneliness and restlessness ... it's so, is not it? ... also melancholies that could have led to an unpleasant madness ... Dr Gomes has perhaps concealed the truth: I'm sure of it ... he was a slothful messenger at times ... bearer of a fatal event without mentioning reasons and sincerities that might have helped me ... ah Mário, Mário lost in desperation: that is what I understood ... Mário forgotten in his madness ... Mário who was unable to narrate to the world the lament of Prometheus ... a Mário de Sá-Carneiro who wished to live in the vanguard, as Dr Gomes reported to me, rather than seek refuge in the ancient world ... Mário frightened ... Mário perhaps suicidal...

– You suppose it then? ... that Dr Gomes implied certainties even in his ambiguous language? ... I am seeking a truth that Senhor Pessoa would like to be confirmed ... reflecting on what has been said: it seems almost an antinomy since Dr Gomes reported to you certainties that only Senhor Pessoa could know ... a drama of intrigue ... ambiguities that rely on light-hearted mind games ... do you understand what I mean? ... saying and not saying or saying so that not saying is also acceptable ... inconsistency of reason ... why? ... conscious madness? ... why then did Senhor Pessoa request this investigation? ... an odd request ... a mad aphorism ... whom to believe? ... voluntary doubts after having given credit to peremptory invitations ...

– ... do not forget the poetry, António Mora interrupted and with an ordinary gesture placed the bundle of folds of his toga on his left shoulder. Then he added: – there is a bizarre sentence pronounced by Dr Gomes, in his elocution, which struck me in particular ... poetry as salvation, he said ... was he referring to Mário de Sá-Carneiro? perhaps ... poetry as a mystery, then ... poetry that is a sublime point of arrival in the ambiguous game of writing ... do you understand? ... it's possible to have fun, or perhaps fiddle about, in a codified manner solemnly affirming one's '*ego*', the mystery of one's '*ego*' ... here then is the poetry that accompanied Mário, according to what Dr Gomes had me understand, in his tragic journey toward the mystery ... yes! a mystery that can sometimes, but not always unfortunately, prevail over death and over madness ... signifying it, then! ... perhaps unwinding that bastard tangle of sentiments drawn from a melancholy desperation ... beginning perhaps to dig into an intimacy that no longer seems to belong ... weaving poetic discourses that were appropriate to whomever had the desire to truly understand that subtle thread of desperation that gripped him ... tearing any ignoble constraint ... playing, as far as was possible, with himself to try to forget the unease of an existence that seemed abominable ... was it really? ... hence poetry seemed to become, at a certain point, truly a possible lifeline ...

He moved away abruptly, almost as if an intuition or a thought urged him to occupy a different space. He stopped on a flat lawn facing the sea. He remained silent for a few seconds. Then he took deep breaths, adjusted several times the toga whose folds were ruffled by a barely perceptible wind. He then seemed to swear, pronouncing words that seemed to be prayers. They were, in truth, only verses from *Prometheus*. Significant desires to give, perhaps, sense to what had been said, to what had been exchanged amid thoughts and desires for knowledge. Perhaps also an epilogue to the encounter with David Mondine? "*Or divine aether, and ye swift-winged breezes, / and ye fountains of rivers, and countless dimpling of the waves of the deep, / and thou earth, mother of all – and to the all-seeing orb of the Sun I appeal*", he repeated then with a rapt air, quoting Aeschylus.

IX

Paris of light, of beauty, of impatience. Paris.

August 1916.

Walking the streets or frequenting a bistro. Pauses for improvised investigations or also for obscure chess problems.

A game of strategies. Life–Death. White–Black. It could not be otherwise.

David Mondine and Dr Abílio Quaresma. Faithful concerning defined pacts and ambiguous agreements. Nothing else. Then waiting for secret meetings. For Mário de Sá-Carneiro, it was said.

Thus it was as it had to be. And how it was guaranteed to be. Arrangements sent by Angus Craston upon the request of Fernando Pessoa. Occasionally, however, rests necessary to restore moods and regenerate forces.

Dr Abílio Quaresma was at the Café de l'Univers at 159 Rue de St-Honoré. He readily joined the players of the *Union Amicale des joueurs de la Régence*, a chess club. He began to puff on a good cigar accompanied by a *Godet* cognac of the "*Maison Godet, négociant en eaux de vie*".

He restored his spirit by exercising his mind. An inveterate visionary of the chessboard in movement. Also going over some unusual moves and acrobatic endings. An essential necessity. Thus concentrating as best possible on the varied information concerning the death of Mário de Sá-Carneiro.

Actions similar to those of Akiba Kiwelowicz Rubinstein, the chess virtuoso who emerged from the ghetto of Stawiski and escaped from the Polish territory that was part of Tsarist Russia. Anthropophobic. Megalomaniac. Paranoid. Akiba Rubinstein walked his own path without yielding to human and social contacts. Modelling his life and his thoughts in the form of a chessboard. Fascinating, Dr Abílio Quaresma must have thought. Manoeuvring as best possible with his Jewish origin, Akiba Kiwelowicz Rubinstein had thought. Each move seemed to have, intentionally, a substantial value of redemption.

David Mondine, accommodated at a small table of the Café Cardinal at 1 Boulevard des Italiens, sipped a *Pastis Ricard* with its fragrance of anise and liquorice. Forgetting, in the fortifying intoxication of alcohol, strenuous treks investigating the traces left by Monsieur Mário de Sá-Carneiro, David Mondine was leafing through a *Baedeker. Paris et ses Environs.* Seizième Édition. 11 Cartes et 32 Plans. 1907. Leipzig Editeur. Not to forget Mário. How could one forget him since he had taken to frequenting Paris? The Café Cardinal seemed suitable for reporting his observations in a letter to Fernando Pessoa. "*Eu amo incomparavelmente mais Paris, eu vejo-o bem mais nitidamente e comprendo-o em bem maior lucidez longe dele, por Lisboa, do que aqui, nos seus boulevardes onde até, confesso-lhe meu Amigo, por vezes eu lhe sou infiel*[87]".

It was certain that Mário had written to Fernando, also on 2 December 1912, regarding his sudden and continuous crises. Melancholies? Unconscious suggestions. Past memories or evanescence of the present? Undoubtedly perverse disquietudes since "*atmosfera, o perfume do ar, a cor do céu, as pessoas que me redor de nós circulam – têm talvez império sobre o nosso estado*[88]". Avid and unrestrained desperation. Death seemed to be standing next to him, insinuated in his mind as a coveted goal. A desire to disappear. Perhaps deep water or a gunshot.

Paris of light, of beauty, of impatience. Paris.

---

87 Letter from Mário de Sá-Carneiro to Fernando Pessoa of 13 July 1914: "*I love Paris incomparably more, I see it much more clearly and understand it with much greater lucidity away from it, in Lisbon, than when here in its boulevards, where at times, my friend, I am unfaithful to you.*"

88 Letter from Mário de Sá-Carneiro to Fernando Pessoa of 2 December 1912: "*the atmosphere, the scent of the air, the colour of the sky, the people we see around us – perhaps dominate our state of mind.*"

* * *

August 1916.

Akiba Rubinstein's moves were always of extraordinary and astonishing audacity. This is what Dr Abílio Quaresma thought to himself, staring at the board. He paid no attention to the chatter surrounding him. The Café de la Régence was crowded. Dr Quaresma had arranged the pieces with self-assurance. Carefully studying the game between Akiba Rubinstein and Gersz Rotlewi. 1907. At Łódź. Checkmate in 25 moves. Move after move with maniacal attention. It did not happen thus for events of a life. Of a childhood above all. Mário de Sá-Carneiro had played a spurious game. Remembering it while Dr Quaresma observed the pieces on the chessboard. Mário was motherless. Playing with impunity without his queen. A check. Certainly evil. Dr Quaresma believed it appropriate to concentrate on the chessboard. Warding off unpleasant thoughts. Above all gossipy rumours. Forgetting what he had learned in Portugal. Now Rubinstein against Rotlewi. Playing with the black pieces was not beneficial. And Akiba Rubinstein played with the blacks. Only exasperating and meticulous rationality. Absolute perfection. Akiba was very clever. Instead Mário had allowed himself to be subdued immediately. He didn't play with either white or black. He was watching a game that nevertheless involved him. Rubinstein was made of different stuff. Yet he was unable to be recognised as world champion. Often he was Mephistophelean. Sharp beyond any legitimate comprehension. An uncrowned emperor. Grandiose combinations. Drawing forth impossible moves from a mind wounded by increasingly severe schizophrenia and full-blown anthropophobia. He was known as the *Immortal.* And Mário? He blundered the opening of his game with life. And it all happened in that first move. It was clear to everyone. Relying on others. Who? The gossipy charlatans reported obscene things. Was it necessary to listen to them? A life in the Chiado[89]. Spending his early childhood there. He was

89 Chiado was one of Lisbon's most traditional districts, between Bairro alto and Baixa.

a rare object. Mário. A kind of prince. A repository of honours. The servants surrounded him with excessive attention. Yet being unable to leave that gilded cage. Hugs and surveillance. Becoming obscenely fat. Gulping down food. A parent had imposed a conservative regime. Massive doses of eggs, red meat and very caloric foods. Obesity was a sign of good health even if in a troubled conscience. Instead Akiba played with firm wisdom. No hugs and no excessive attention for him. Alone. Yet resisting with extreme wisdom against external solicitations. He was facing Gersz Rotlewi. Opening with d4 (white) and d5 (black). So it was that Akiba began to dominate. A maestro's move. With black or white, it didn't matter. Obliging the white to exchange a pawn. A repertoire studied in the smallest detail. A winning repertoire. The black pieces seemed to become bizarre conquerors of the board. Akiba played with black. An open and violent confrontation. Sacrificing in order to harmoniously position his pieces. And Dr Quaresma remained engrossed in understanding why Akiba Rubinstein had made that move with a firm hand.

* * *

August 1916.

Unbearable mugginess. However, it was enough to live with a few francs, so it was said. Indeed 15 or 20 francs were sufficient. Mário had written so. Also a city of distractions, if one wished. Paris. City of ancient lineages. It was worth remembering it. David Mondine slavishly followed a *Baedeker.* Referring everything to the course of history. Merovingians and Carolingians. Then the Louis kings. Up to the eighteenth century. Not beyond. Impossible, in fact. The guillotine cut short the Bourbon dynasty of France. Then revolution and restoration. Mondine enjoyed reading about the events in a café. Sipping a *Pastis Ricard.* Surrounded by beautiful people. La Ville Lumière. However, Mário had wandered the city with distressing melancholy. Spare of experiences and initiatives. Forced to frequent, often reluctantly, Portuguese riff-raff. He frequented them necessarily.

There was nothing else to do. *"E essa gente? Lacerda, Beirões, Santa-Rita, Ponce, Ferro... heterogénea mistura!*[90]*"* indeed. He was struck by the *"idea da saudade antes da posse que eu acho qualquer coisa de trágico e grande – ter saudade já do futuro*[91]*"*. Writing poems recovering desperate memories. All the memories for which he was aware that they were such. Yet so much rancour. So much despair. Paris was a beautiful city, no doubt. Therefore, it was reasonable to declare that it was a wonder that shone in all its gold, in a kind of imponderable, subtle, feverish spell. As one glanced around, it also seemed a city with disturbing ambiguities. Visiting places and indulging in reflections. The *Baedeker* also provided David Mondine with disappointments. Instructions for use. What could ever be balanced knowledge? An inveterate habit. Habits acquired through descendance. Paris the eccentric was a temptress city. At least it was thought so. A city that seemed to be smiling, so much so that it seemed to Mário that there was *"um fiozinho de esperança que todas as aspirações dentro de mim me fizeram ver como um facho resplandecente*[92]*"*. Certain however of moving toward a devastating disappointment. A mish-mash from which it seemed difficult to exit. Prisoner of a city? Meanwhile, the zeppelins bombed the city, while at the Folies Bergère the women danced frenetically and Mistinguett sang *Mon Homme*. *"Sur cette terr', ma seul' joie, mon seul bonheur / C'est mon homme. / J'ai donné tout c'que j'ai, mon amour et tout mon cœur / À mon homme.*[93]*"*

Paris of light, of beauty, of impatience. Paris.

---

90 Letter from Mário de Sá-Carneiro to Fernando Pessoa of 21 January 1913: *"And these people? Lacerda, Beirões, Santa-Rita, Ponce, Ferro... a heterogeneous mixture."*

91 Letter from Mário de Sá-Carneiro to Fernando Pessoa of 3 February 1913. *"idea of nostalgia before finding something tragic and grand – already being nostalgic of the future."*

92 Letter from Mário de Sá-Carneiro to Fernando Pessoa of 16 November 1912: *"a small strand of hope that all the aspirations inside me made me see a resplendent light."*

93 *"On this earth, my only joy, my only happiness / It's my man / I give everything I have, my love and my heart / To my man."*

* * *

August 1916.

Dr Quaresma was immobile in front of the chessboard. Gazing at the move that Akiba had made in that fateful game. Gersz Rotlewi was not an easy opponent. Both Jews from Łódź. Of different ages. Akiba born in 1882. Gersz in 1889. Both brilliant. Jews were brilliant chess players. Emanuel Lasker, Richard Réti and Wilhelm Steinitz famous Jewish cryptographers. Also Gersz Rotlewi. Also Akiba Rubinstein. Study and perseverance. Quick to learn languages. A code of communication, in short. Chess was nothing but a coded language. The game seemed to suddenly open up. White, then. White could no longer commit errors. It could absolutely not. Gersz Rotlewi had to be more careful. The queen, then. The queen poorly positioned. Black was better positioned. It resumed without advantages or disadvantages. Akiba and Gersz at the same level. Then Mário came to mind. A sip of *Godet* cognac to regenerate his spirit. Taking his eyes off the board. Why had Mário become a panderer of a game of life? Embalmed, in fact. Standing there gazing at men and things. A lack of courage in facing the world? Still young, certainly. Self-taught when reading began to accompany him assiduously. At Livararia Ferreira – Rua Aurea 132-138. Or at Livraria Mónaco – Praça Dom Pedro. Despising rash attitudes. Also indifference and carelessness. Distant from him. Distant from what seemed as if it did not belong to any culture. What? Akiba and Gersz played with brilliant intelligence. The Baixa, the chic district near the Praça do Commercio, instead marked the borders of imbecility. Indeed, the stupidity of that prosperous middle class that lived there was rampant. Appealing then to his own intimate dignity. Not looking in the mirror. Iniquitous indicator. A resolute ugliness was reflected as a truthful image. Fat and soft. Also a lost look, hard face, pursed lips. An intimate and despotic drama. Accepting his existence? Thus he began to despise humanity. Meanwhile, Gersz was forced to move the white. Dr Quaresma abruptly gulped another glass of *Godet* cognac, concentrating once again on the chessboard.

* * *

The month was the same, also the year.

Meanwhile, a monument was attracting attention. Wrought iron. Steel mills working full out. Forging and shaping. Total weight: 7300 tonnes. Height: 312.27 metres. Four foundations supported the construction. A fideist liturgy facing the four cardinal points. Liturgy? *Sacrum facere.* Dignity. Great Endeavour. In the form of a Quaternary (the Masonic symbol of the Eternal and Creative Principle). The four essential elements. Earth–water–air–fire. The rite was the prerogative of the adepts. Sectarian obedience. A *Baedeker* could certainly not provide clarification. Just a tower, it was written. A simple tower. 1792 steps. Distinguished work of the engineer Alexandre Gustave Eiffel. Bearded. Wavy hair. Elegantly dressed. Lovely large bow tie. 1889 World's Fair. Cost: 41 and a half million francs. Astonishing admiration for such indecent audacity. Also for the unusually high cost. Painful the adverse opinions. *"Odious column of bolted tin." "Absolutely tragic lamp post." "Factory smokestack."* Ingenuous judgments? Only misguided opinions. Superficial people of limited intelligence. Riff-raff, perhaps. Guy de Maupassant and Alexandre Dumas *fils.* Instead Mário de Sá-Carneiro seemed enchanted by that wrought iron. A mind marked by neglect and by reckless will. An exile: it was certain. Haunting the streets without destination. Reading with amazement about that iron tower. What could be expected from imaginary engineering propositions? *"A minha Alma, fugiu pela Torre Eiffel acima, / – A verdade é esta, não nos criemos mais ilusões / – Fugiu, mas foi apanhada pela antena da TSF / Que a transmitiu pelo infinito em ondas hertzianas*[94]*"*, Mário had written in a letter to his friend Fernando. Yet he was often wrong in wishing to deceive himself. Prerogative of unconscious irrationality. Mário had not been happy in that ideal city because

94 2 August 1915: *"My soul has fled onto the Eiffel Tower. That is the truth, let us not create any more illusions. It has fled, but it has been captured by the TSF antenna, which has sent it through infinity in the radio waves."*

he seemed to be living some of the worst days of his life. Many recriminations tormented him. Many nostalgias. Indeed, a profound nostalgia consumed him, forced him to feel a melancholic sadness. Nostalgia for all that he had experienced, the deceased people he had esteemed and who had loved him. Suffering in this way and with impunity for the strangest and most incomprehensible things: for things that had never happened, for "*a saudade de todos as coisas que vivi, as pessoas desaparecidas que estimei e foram carinhosas para mi... a morte fatal e próxima de algumas pessoas que estimo profundamente e são idosas*[95]".

Paris of light, of beauty, of impatience. Paris.

* * *

Still August 1916.

Paying attention, Dr Abílio Quaresma narrowed his eyes slightly. To better understand Akiba's subtle and reckless brilliance. Akiba continuously reinforced his strategy. He increased slowly, but with rigour, his endgame strategy. A sip of *Godet* cognac. To bolster the spirit. To clear the mind. Also a cigar. Dr Quaresma lit it with indolent delight. He used two matches since the first went out in his hand. Maximum attention to the chessboard. Tenth move. White queen in d2. Akiba the virtuoso certainly watched Gersz's move with smug serenity. Akiba of the countless potentialities. Akiba of incomparable technical preparation. Dr Quaresma lustily inspired the cigar smoke. Superb. Excellent advice from the owner of the À la Civette tobacco shop at 157 Rue St. Honoré. The Commander was of fine workmanship. Tenth move. White queen in d2. Dr Quaresma looked slyly at the chessboard. He was at ease. He seemed to reside in Paris with an insatiable security. Instead Mário had begun to travel and move away from Lisbon with a neurotic tone. His father,

95 Letter from Mário de Sá-Carneiro to Fernando Pessoa of 16 November 1912. *"the nostalgia for all the things that I've experienced, for the deceased persons I've cherished and who cared for me ... for the fatal and proximal death of some people whom I profoundly esteem and are elderly."*

Carlos Augusto, was not an ideal companion. Dr Quaresma had obtained certain information about those events. At the age of 11, Mário had gone on holiday. A chalet. At Povoa de Varzim. A fishing village on the Costa Verde, south of Oporto. Acquiring a tiresome monotony. He observed what was happening around him. Especially at the Café Chinês with Spanish singers. Disconcerting puberty. The nausea of being himself. He became lost in disheartening considerations. Then he found himself alone. Onan often comforted him. Shivers of exasperating pleasure. Akiba also must have experienced a disconcerting emotion looking at the chessboard. Rotlewi's tenth move was terribly fatal. The white queen was now positioned poorly. It seemed that Gersz Rotlewi had lost all hope. Akiba avoided the move d5xc4 so as not to help Rotlewi save his queen. Dr Quaresma smiled. He took a puff on his cigar and moved the black as Akiba had done.

* * *

Still Paris, still the same month and year.

David Mondine was wandering about Paris with the *Baedeker* in his hands. Experiencing a day of sightseeing now that he was satisfied by senseless and tiresome investigations. Wandering, in fact. First refreshing himself in a brasserie. An affordable menu. *Entrée: filet de hareng a 1 franc et 50 cents. Plat: Steak hache sauce poivre vert frites a 7 francs et 50 cents. Fromage: Saint nectaire a 2 francs. Dessert: Coupe de creme chantilly a 2 francs.* Slightly higher prices than those indicated by the *Baedeker.*

Finally finding himself, comforted by the food, walking streets just beyond Boulevard Saint Germain. Travelling routes enclosed within a geometric shape. A trapezoid, it seemed. On the *Baedeker* map, the outline was unmistakable. At a glance there was la Monnaie[96] with its long facade. Reading the notes in the guide. Ionic columns. Also allegorical statues. Then a corner,

96 *La Monnaie* is the national mint of France.

in Rue Buci des Arts, that led in two directions. Rue Mazarine and Rue Dauphine. Inside, alleyways. A tangled maze. Or so it seemed. Never retracing his steps if he wished to exit from that maze in good time. A certain way out: Quai Conti. Then following the left bank of the Seine. Then returning whence he came. Then along Rue Mazarine. A necessary visit since he had time to spend as best possible. The Institut de France, as the *Baedeker* advised. Instructions for use. More than necessary descriptions. But appropriate. Especially the library: 250,000 volumes, 1900 incunabula, 5800 amanuenses. Splendid bronze busts. Magnificent pendulum clocks and models of Pelasgian monuments. Why then did Mário feel disoriented when crossing Rue Mazarine? Terrible affair. Was it possible to dawdle, dismayed, and feel frozen in front of a road that led to a library? Rue Mazarine like Bairro Alto? This is what he wrote in a letter. Almost ancient phantasms that roamed about annoyingly. And the memories caused a distressing, demeaning, humiliating sadness; a sadness of yellowish complexion. He wasn't at all at the Igreja do Carmo as Mário had written. In front of that ghost church. The remembrances were precious memories. Immutable. Also recollecting excrement and rats that marked the roads and hid among imposing ruins. The library was another thing. Did he wander, then, to find himself once again in Lisbon? Anxiously seeking Lisbon? Lisbon in his heart. Not being able to forget it. Looking back and affirming, as Mário wrote, that "*os tempos a que eu chamei desventurados, afiguramse-me hoje áureos, suaves e neneficos*[97]". The same frequentations, then, in that of Paris. A foreign land but Portuguese acquaintances. The Institut de France was, in fact, ignored by Mário listening to the little tunes strummed on guitars which were certainly not *fados.*

Paris of light, of beauty, of impatience. Paris.

* * *

97 Letter from Mário de Sá-Carneiro to Fernando Pessoa of 16 November 1912 *"the times I once called wretched now seem to me golden, sweet and happy."*

August 1916.

The game had arrived at the 22nd move. Dr Quaresma remained stunned for a few moments staring at the chessboard. He took a long puff on his third Commander as he began avidly to smoke. Akiba Rubinstein undoubtedly displayed an unequalled genius. Reflecting. Reflecting on what? Akiba was intuitive and imaginative. His greatness was never fully recognised. It was then that Dr Quaresma could only think of Mário. Another genius lost in the determination to be forgotten? An unfortunate life. That was certain. A pilgrim without a destination and with the desire to live in a place that was not a physical place. Lisbon or Paris? Performing as if he were the Wandering Jew. Denying any welcome and leaving. Evil eschatology. Did Mário perhaps boast of Jewish ancestry? Like Akiba, after all. Better then to dramatise his existence. Bending, as need be, to the love of someone similar to him. Fernando had shown himself to be a master of habits and mystifications. Akiba Rubinstein had also been a master. The 23rd move had been the result of a subtle and daring intellectual cogitation. Reflecting. Thinking with discernment. Fernando, meanwhile, was a repository of unique fantasies. For Mário, he had been the master of suspense and instability. Also the only person with whom he felt the desire to "*encostar a cabeça ao deu braço – e de o ter aqui, ao pé de mim, como gostaria de ter o meu Pai, a minha Ama ou qualquer objecto, qulquer bicho querido da infância*[98]!" Akiba had by now put Gersz Rotlewi in serious difficulty. White was about to capitulate. Mário had offered himself as a sacrificial lamb. A terrible story, thought Dr Quaresma.

* * *

98 Letter from Mário de Sá-Carneiro to Fernando Pessoa of 13 July 1914: *"rest my head on his arm and have him here next to me, as I would like to have my father, my wet nurse or some object, some beloved pet from my childhood."*

Still August 1916.

The letter was from 3 April of that year. 1916, in fact. Death was lurking. Mário's words. His friend Pessoa had read those alarming revelations. Subtle and intriguing signals. Ambiguity of a fiction or fiction of an ambiguity? *"Adeus, meu querido Fernando Pessoa. É hoje segunda-feira 3 que morro atirando-me para debaixo do 'Métro' (ou melhor do 'Nord-Sud') na estação de Pigalle.*[99]*"* Line 2: from Place de la Nation to Porte Dauphine. An announcement of death so that death would not ensue? Save or be saved? An accusal as well? Even a challenge. Mário was trained to offer disturbing extortions. Real death or imagined death? Perhaps also a madness that was now corroding. The Pigalle Station could well have been a place of solitude and disequilibrium. This, perhaps, is what David Mondine was thinking. Visiting that place. Also the surroundings. Exploratory necessities. Perceiving sensations of streets and inhabitants. As far as Place de Clichy? Thus feeling impulses of past wills and past events. A land of conquest, so it suddenly seemed. Hence David Mondine visited those places. Why had Mário chosen the Metro at Pigalle? Madness filled the air. Mário and others. Glancing around. Going and going. Almost like a bloodhound. The encounter happened by chance. Alleys that wound toward the Butte Montmartre. Shabby bistros. Small hotels for a few cents per night. Louts with a bad reputation. Sordid prostitutes. Backrooms like opium dens. Outdoor urinals. Sleazy stenches of filthy bodies. A humanity lost in obscene degradation. Also encountering chronic drunkenness. Bottle in hand and incomprehensible babbling. Life and death. Then a man with delicate features. He appeared suddenly. Shunned, ridiculed, avoided. Maurice Utrillo walked the streets with reckless disequilibrium. Alcohol, then. Encountering him inebriated. He was also marked by schizophrenia. Painting as the only therapy. An asylum at the ready. Entering and exiting

99 Letter from Mário de Sá-Carneiro to Fernando Pessoa of 3 April 1916: *"Adieu, my dear Fernando Pessoa. Today, Monday the 3rd, I will kill myself by throwing myself under the 'Métro' (or better the 'North-South') in the Pigalle station."*

rooms enclosed by bars. Then rushing back to the streets. To be insulted once again. Shabby and short-tempered. Crouching in dark corners and sucking on wine. Saving himself. Mondine seemed to see him lost in mad dreams. Going, going without destination or desire. Rash actions. Even throwing knives. Last opportunities, by now. The air disturbed him because many ridiculed him. Sooner or later, Maurice would be confined to a studio to continue painting Montmartre street corners. An unfortunate fate. The postcards would become extraordinary pictorial panoramas. The wine seemed merely a plenary indulgence. Life of a vagabond, of a protagonist of scandals. Fleeing from his disquietudes. Swigging from the neck of each bottle as long as it contained wine. Thus his nickname '*litrillo*'. Also protagonist of extraordinary touches. Oils, watercolours and gouaches. Working tirelessly. Had Mário ever met him? Pigalle had been horribly tempting. Yet on 3 April 1916 no suicide was foreseen.

Paris of light, of beauty, of impatience. Paris.

* * *

August 1916.

Smoking nonstop. Even a few glasses of cognac. To finish the game. To pay tribute to Akiba Rubinstein. Unparalleled genius. Never proud. Discretion and maximal respect for the opponent. Pathological shyness. Perhaps it was madness that was making its way into Akiba's mind. Studying until he dropped. Opening and closing moves. Unique chess strategies. Ending the game with Gersz Rotlewi. Dr Quaresma remained staring at the chessboard for a few moments. A sip of cognac. A puff on the Commander. 24th move: it would be remembered as *the immortal*. Perhaps Mário also sought immortality with a single act. Suicide or something else? Providing appropriate responses to Fernando Pessoa. A cry of pain. Begging as well. Wishing to die in silence or wishing to be saved by silence? Pleading. Playing with literature up to the end. Was this the desire to say goodbye?

Undoubtedly he considered that his "*doença moral é terrível – diversa e novamente complicada a cada instante*[100]". A dark desire. To commit suicide? Gersz Rotlewi had also committed suicide with that reckless move. Dr Quaresma smiled with pleasure. Inevitable abandonment by white. Another sip of cognac. And another puff on the *Commander*. Rh3. Adieu! Suicide?

* * *

Same month and year. Also the city.

Gallivanting on les boulevards. Between the Café Cardinal Restaurant and the Café Riche there was always a preened Monsieur immersed in reading *Le Temps*. Life seemed to flow oblivious of any tragedy. Not of himself, certainly. Automobiles, carriages and the crowd thronged on the broad sidewalks. There it was possible to detect laboured breaths, laden with tension as if they were violin chords. Mário spent his days solacing himself by observing the passers-by, writing to Fernando, reading the newspapers. News, then. David Mondine thought it appropriate to take note of the daily events. Of Paris and of France. What was happening? Thus he began to read the newspapers available there as in any café. Reading only the headlines on the front page. Extracting news summaries. *Le Figaro*: 734th day of war. On the right bank of the Meuse the enemy has not made any other attack on Thiaumont-Verdun. The Germans were pushed back six times during the night. Thiaumont suffocated by terrible bombing. *L'Humanité*: Our soldiers retain the Ouvrage de Thiaumont and are still fighting at Village de Fleury. The battalion of the 241 Infantry Regiment maintains the position on the south side and prevents any enemy sortie. Unprecedented massacres. *L'Intransigeant*: In the region of Fleury the artillery has continued to fire without the intervention of the infantry. The German General Erich von Falkenhayn is attempting to "*bleed*

100 Letter from Mário de Sá-Carneiro to Fernando Pessoa of 17 April 1916: *"moral disease is terrible – different and again complicated at every moment."*

drop by drop" the French army. *L'Homme Libre*: Aerial war. Raid on Ghent. Four German planes shot down. The German Air Force has abandoned the military and industrial targets to hit major civilian centres. Hundreds dead. *Le Matin*: the 179th Tunnelling Company Royal Engineers, which had dug a tunnel to arrive under the German stronghold of Pozières, called '*Schwaben Höhe*', 1 July, at 07:28, detonated a mine that caused a huge blast and a column of smoke and debris that rose into the air for circa 1200 metres. Thus began the offensive to break through the German lines for a distance of circa 60 kilometres between Lassigny and Hébuterne. *Le Siècle*: German ferocity. The regime imposed on the occupied Belgian provinces is very harsh. The governor Moritz Ferdinand von Bissing is operating with fierce determination to separate the Flemish provinces from the Walloon ones and make the former a German protectorate. Civilian casualties have been 5000 thus far. Also summary executions. For having committed acts judged to be illegal. *Le Temps*: The battle was hard, violent and bloody north of Verdun. Severe losses. The past few months have seen 126,000 deaths in the German army and 133,000 in the French one. Phosgene gas, that is carbonyl dichloride gas, is being used indiscriminately by the Germans. The soldiers experience sudden sickness due to suffocation accompanied by coughing, nausea, vomiting and headaches. The condition of the soldiers is aggravated when they are subjected to forced marches or hand-to-hand combat. Chemical warfare is something atrociously unimaginable.

– My God, David Mondine said troubled. He left the newspapers thrown together haphazardly on a table and forgot Mário for a moment.

X

Reordering a life. Investigating a death. Essential tasks. With inflexible authority, Angus Craston and Fernando Pessoa prescribed that I undertake them. Thus I followed paths meant to reconstruct a life and verify a death. A damaged life, an ambiguous death.

Mário de Sá-Carneiro, son of Lisbon, died here in Paris. A terrible story, without doubt. Thus I scoured this city inch by inch. Even with unexpected distractions and necessary pauses. Reordering the mind. Regenerating the body. Enormous fatigue in prolonged treks. This must be recognised. I will keep it in mind when I draft the final reports on my investigation. A difficult task, however.

Mário was little known in Paris: that is certain. Few remember him. Few exchanged words and confidences with him. Mário seemed to have been a shadow-man. He fled from friendships. He avoided facing reality. A doctor, whom I met by chance in the Pâtisserie Bourbonneux, at 14 Place du Havre, and who had acquired some information about Mário through an intermediary, provided a mental profile talking of schizophrenia.

Mário was, according to him, very similar to a child and to a dreamer who could not live in reality. He was very unreasonable and devoid of all common sense. Even lacking all the requirements that define human nature. His behaviour showed, incontrovertibly, a false rebellion that signified an inevitable rupture with some types of socialisation, the most important and necessary ones.

Moreover, he took refuge in claustrophobic dreams. Information also confirmed by people met with discretion and subjected, cautiously on my part, to inquisitorial desires once I had heard the unfortunate diagnosis by that doctor. I spoke about Mário wherever it was possible to exchange words and intentions. In locales in particular. I frequented many of them. *Cafés, brasseries, patisseries, thées.* In many of these places I consumed syrups of a repulsive sugary flavour. No alcohol I promised myself, at least in the morning and early afternoon.

The mind had to be ready to receive news and information. I even attended places unusual for me: *bains chaud et froids, coiffeurs, cabinets inodores,* in other words *les chalets de nécessite et de commodité.* I walked the *boulevards,* the *places,* the *rues,* the *gares.* I frequented *la station de voitures de place e de remis* in Rue Haley. With cruel malice and unexpected ruthlessness, I interrogated the owners of *hôtels* of the lowest order where I imagined that Mário might have found temporary hospitality when he was not staying in those boarding houses whose addresses were supplied, indirectly, by Fernando Pessoa.

While I was trekking about Paris, Dr Abílio Quaresma, for all that he had to do, played his part as a *sui generis* and odd investigator. He was tolerant and tranquil in his singular role as insightful and indulgent companion. Sufficient to keep him interested in and alert to this investigation were an elegant chessboard, full glasses of good cognac or various liquors of high alcohol content, and fragrant cigars. Very good the *Commanders,* he murmured, even though they were not the *Peraltas* he preferred and sometimes longed for.

At the end of the day, we met in some bistro to take stock of my investigations and to plan how to spend my time the following day. We frequented many bistros. Thus we began to pass the nights choosing the locales that offered liquors of good taste and low price: often mixed with strange alcoholic essences. A criticism we expressed immediately because nothing escaped our palates.

Precious merchandise and sublime distillation according to the owners of the bistros. *Absinthe, Armagnac, Raki, Izarra Jaune,*

Elixir Combier, Anisette Marie Brizard. From 40 to 70 percent alcohol. Many herbs. Many fragrances. Many mixtures. But above all sugar and aromas that were not at all natural. Spurious additions, in fact. Even the criminal *Illicium verum*[101]. One swig after another without any shame so that our mandate might seem less grim.

Dr Quaresma heard about my daily wanderings between one sip and another, already shamelessly intoxicated with liquor and often exhausted by his obsessive reconstruction of a famous chess game. Rubinstein vs. Rotlewi: an unrivalled game. The game of the century: a justification of his time squandered in front of a chessboard. He shook his head agreeing with suitable regret. In my opinion, he understood little of what he was saying to himself, albeit ready to reply with opinions and ideas in an attempt to reconstruct, in his own way, a story that seemed to elude us, since the mind, a little after sunset, was often clouded by abundant libations.

A mystery, he muttered from time to time as if to appease me and to induce in me a strong anguish about our investigative inefficacy.

Busy as we were with an investigation for which we had the obligation to provide plausible solutions, we fell into a spiral of carelessness that proved to be a grave insult to our intelligence.

All around there was something else. *Il faut tenir*[102], was said with a firm voice. *On les aura*[103], was replied with equal firmness. All around were occurring events that escaped us even though we felt that the Parisians, who perceived them with detached worry and impassive trepidation, preferred not to talk about them with the attention they deserved.

The comings and goings of soldiers was very evident as was our encountering war wounded marked by permanent disfigurement and *poilus*[104] covered in mud and dirt from head to toe. Because of a strong unawareness, involved as we were in

---

101 Star anise.

102 *One mustn't give up.*

103 *We'll get them.*

104 Hairy ones.

researches as investigative hacks, and also because we were drunk with fatigue and liquors, we did not understand that a dreadful tragedy was taking on devastating proportions all around us. The newspapers, it is true, speak about it and provide news corrected and dictated by the ambiguous wills of the rulers and the high military men. The newspapers are read but forgotten within a few hours because they tell stories that do not seem to belong to the reality of everyday life despite the tragic nature of the news.

Soldiers are only phantasms if mentioned in simple bulletins and dispatches which soon become merely statistics calculated to count the dead and seriously injured, as if they were units of measures. Pure and simple statistics. Hence it was necessary not to notice a reality that did not seem real. A carnage that was almost habitual and thus forgettable. Few questions were posed in the bistros. Are we winning or losing, one wonders, almost as if it were a football match. The enemy has broken through our rearguard, almost as if it were a rugby match. Our frontline is advancing or is dug in, almost as if it were a chess game.

Fears wilfully assimilated, so much so that it was pleasant to be in the city and not at any war front. Nothing else, then! It also seemed to me, according to collected gossip, that Mário never perceived a looming tragedy that was shaking France.

Mário with his chronic oddities. Mário who went about the city bundled up in melancholy and shy solitude. Mário who believed it necessary to inflict heartache upon himself to atone for his dark irreverences. Mário who played the part of a fashionable anti-conformist. Mário who was so self-absorbed that he seemed to live in a constant dreamlike delirium. Mário who seemed to want to be surrounded by an atmosphere of non-involvement and thus to enjoy his disquietude. Mário who was afraid to retrace his steps because nothing could ever be the same as before. Mário who wallowed in his contemplative ecstasy because the rest was extraneous to him. Mário who complacently felt that he did not belong to any city or country. Mário who was extremely concerned about the dark sensations of his instinct. Mário who considered his mind able to create an inappropriate reality disturbing to the society he was compelled to endure. Mário who complained of a nostalgia which, in truth, he did not feel because no nostalgia could satisfy him. Mário who wasted time in remembrances that responded to memories recovered from a reality experienced in a distorted manner and never loved. Mário who wished to construct a world in his own image and likeness, even though an innate discontent forced him to presume that there could never be a world in his image and likeness. Mário who was tirelessly seeking a fictitious gratification of his intimate desires which seemed to him impossible on account of that kind of apathy in which he delighted in living. Mário who seemed to have a poor ability to reflect realistically about himself and his fantasies because he was a simple dreamer who did not wish to realise any dream. Mário who exhibited, according to many who knew him, a strong affective deficit and a smug reluctance to establish cordial friendships. Mário who seemed to feel the irrepressible desire to influence the world, to be a protagonist as a poet and playwright. Mário who had a true servile propensity for Pessoa, for which he was ready to satisfy any request or desire merely to please him. Mário who was aroused by any challenge to authorities and conventions, to the point of paying for such challenges with a frustrating interior disorder. Mário who, according to people who often met him but who were, it seemed to me, not completely reliable, often had a blank look while gazing in shop windows or mirrors, almost as if he did not distinguish his own reflection. Mário who at times seemed not to recognize what was usual, whereas he believed that he knew someone or something he had never known. Mário who often felt himself a prisoner of a tragic sensation in which reality seemed bizarrely unalterable, almost motionless and indestructible. Mário who was sometimes prey to an anguish he could not decipher, almost as if it were a profound malaise so intimate and personal that it could not be understood in any way or with any language of the mind. Mário who was certainly aware of how misleading were the appearances of daily life, so that he had the sensation that everything around him was inexplicably ambiguous. Mário who often believed that he felt a deep separation between himself and others, so that each of his acts could not be modulated to what others did or thought to do. Mário who felt himself a prisoner of continuous compulsive actions, bringing into play his consciousness, wondering for example if his behaviour was acceptable or not, so much so that he considered it appropriate to acknowledge this, by means of letters, to Fernando Pessoa. Mário who was regularly hesitant about choosing and not choosing, taken as he was by strong motivations that drove him to act and also by apathetic wills that readily rendered him slothful, so that he was incapable of dealing with the usual aspects and ordinary hardships of daily life. Mário who could not accept his own body and thus tried to conceal his emotions, obliged to reveal them only through eccentric intellectual elaborations. Mário who occasionally felt a certain detachment from himself, so that his actions might have appeared illogical, unmotivated and self-destructive. Mário who perhaps had sought his own identity.

It was then that the notes Angus Craston had sent to me in some memoranda came to mind. Philosophical summaries of thinkers who had ventured to clarify the meaning of *"identity"*. Thales of Miletus, Parmenides of Elea, Anaximander of Miletus, Plotinus of Lycopolis and Heraclitus of Ephesus. Extraordinary geniuses who had meditated on the meaning to be given to the definition of *"identity"*.

Mário had nothing to do, on account of his bizarre life in perennial search for an identity that could belong to him, with philosophical intuitions that viewed *"identity"* as a set of unequals, or as compliant with diversity, or as a constituent of the indefinite, or even as a *unicum* born of many, or, finally, as a variation of one's being.

Mário, then! He seemed not to want to have a precise identity.

Mário de Sá-Carneiro.

Mário who lived in Paris and died there in an unusual manner. He left few traces. Very few friends. Only the places he frequented could provide me with foolish whispers. Gossipy voices. Malicious chatter. Mário lost in his melancholic vices and in his anomalous virtues. Mário, in fact.

To my guide, Abílio Quaresma, I reported only appropriate certainties so that he could possess logical continuities from which to draw a plausible solution to the intrigue. Nothing, in fact, can be more fragile than the human mind and nothing is conceded to the free will of those who have the mind and the distinction to investigate the fragility of the mind.

Dr Quaresma will certainly be very capable of providing our client, Mr Craston, and thus indirectly Fernando Pessoa, with precise and honest verbal accounts that are satisfactory conclusions to our investigation.

For my part, I consulted, in order to give a coherent sense to the investigation, José Araújo who was a close acquaintance of Mário and who seems to conserve intuitive secrets concerning the last days of Mário's life. Araújo, who is a kind of salesman, has a Portuguese origin and the facility with which he makes himself available for disinterested friendships. He has beliefs pertinent to his way of life so that, also regarding Mário, he reported to me opinions that may well have a certain basis.

Moreover, José Araújo is the only one who could provide us with certain information that otherwise we could not have obtained. He held forth with pride. Perhaps Mario had been involved with a woman, he explained to me with somewhat unconvincing words.

A woman, then.

A prostitute in search of momentaneous and sudden encounters because, at present, in Paris there is a shortage of men willing to frequent the whores, who thus need to scrape together a few cents in order to survive. Mário was an easy prey and became a slave of his ineptitude and his psychological fragility.

José Araújo asserted this with specific security, providing me with a story that I believe should be reported without any corrections. The meeting between Mário and the prostitute occurred in a café. Perhaps the Café Cyrano, in Place Blanche, or perhaps in another bistro in Montmartre. Locales that Mário frequented by exasperating habit. Mário consumed the hours there writing to his friend Fernando or lazing in melancholy waiting for something to placate his disquietude and grant him moments of cautious existence.

Sometimes, in despair, he sent anguished missives to his father requesting economic aid of which indeed, according to José Araújo, he had no urgent need but which he pretended to have merely to attract attention. He also wrote to his grandfather but they were letters of affection, bound as he was to the old José Paulino who lived in Camarate, a place that Mário remembered fondly when he wrote to Pessoa: "*minhas lágrimas que unicamente assomam vão, longinquamente, para as ruas de minha quinta quando eu tinha cinco anos, e o leito pequeno de ferro em que eu dormia*[105]".

A woman, in a March evening, upset Mário's established habits and precarious desire to silently yield to his restlessness. He felt sorry for himself and, with sharp and distressing words, he informed his friend Fernando. He wrote almost to appease himself, pouring onto the page sentiments that he felt or that he thought he felt when analysing his life. Suddenly there appeared a woman, according to José Araújo.

Was Hélène the name of that woman who despotically entered into Mário's life? It seems that Mário welcomed her after hesitant uncertainties as an unexpected salvation since, on 31 March 1916, he wrote to Fernando: "*Vivo há 15 dias uma vida como sempre sonhei: tive tudo durante eles: realizada a parte sexual, enfim, de minha obra – vivido o histerismo do seu ópio, as luas zebradas, os mosqueiros roxos da sua ilusão*[106]".

José Araújo was convinced that Mário became fascinated with the anomalous singularity of being chatted up by a woman

---

105 Letter of 13 July 1914: *"the tears that appear in my eyes remembering the roads of my farmhouse when I was five years old, that small iron bed where I slept."*

106 *"I've lived for 15 days a life as I've always dreamed it: I've had everything during them: realised the sexual part, finally, of my work – experienced the hysteria of her opium, the zebra moons, the purple gnats of her illusion."*

of easy virtue and by being able to experience unexpected nights of love. Thus also frequenting vices. Many vices. Letting himself go without recriminating about what might happen when it seemed that something had necessarily to happen. José Araújo was rather unpersuaded in reporting his states of mind.

Why did Mário have to submit, once subjugated, to the rash vagaries of a young woman who often caused him physical and moral pains and who often forced him to sniff ether? Oblivion sought and generated by the negligence of being what he was? José Araújo came up with singular interpretations. Convoluted reasonings. Going well beyond any recrimination.

Was Mário a conscious liar? Would a hungry woman of delinquent physical insolence have had an interest in fatally wounding a man whom she accompanied and from whom she received peculiar benefits? Madness? Mário wanted to hide his inner pain. Mário aspired to conquer suicide, if suicide it was, when an abstruse and incomprehensible madness had obsessively taken over his mind, tyrannised him, imposed on him an end that was manifestly eccentric. A sought end. At whose hands?

A misunderstood author. A conscious or unconscious act?

Someone had presided over his mind. Mário was lost in complex machinations that measured out moods and nostalgias. Nostalgia for what?

José Araújo evaded this question when I posed it to him. José Araújo is a tenacious protector of a friend's memory. But José Araújo also has to justify himself for not being on time for an appointment with a foretold death. Thus with me he hid behind an initial and obstinate penance. He was silent. Then he murmured obscure words. Having to relive a pain. An ugly spectacle, he finally said in a faint voice. Ugly spectacle, he repeated. Then he began to shower me with remembrances.

Hôtel de Nice. 26 April 1916.

The man was lying on the bed in formal dress. Five phials of strychnine on display. The photo of a woman on the night table. Slow, atrocious agony. A desired death amidst excruciating, unbearable pain. And José Araújo, late to his appointment with

Mário, was distraught at his imprudence in having to witness the death of a friend who perhaps had wanted to be saved. While he was wasting time, Mário's ambiguous desire to demonstrate that it was possible to put an end to one's days in an eccentric manner was satisfied. Carrying out a spectacular act that defined an often declared, but perhaps never really desired, death wish.

Thus time had been an inexorable avenger, reining José Araújo into events of his typical dawdling.

José Araújo showed great pity for himself. Then he expressed perplexity. Justifying himself in some way since he told me that he did not know, in truth, if that death had really occurred by Mário's hand. Did José Araújo really need to atone for blatant neglect?

José Araújo began to reel off prior events that might justify that death caused perhaps by indirect reasons and unfortunate occasions. Above all by a woman. By that woman. José Araújo singled out Hélène. Barely mumbled words. Ideas that came to him instantly. He spoke with harsh tones, with absurd motivations, with ambiguous premises. Mário seemed to have fallen into the trap of a sexuality never before experienced. Certainly Mário, with mental arrogance, had had masochistic dreams. Also writings in which perversion was the subtly distinctive element. Frustrating loves without ever having experienced love.

Then that woman, Hélène, had certainly seemed the embodiment of long desired dreams. Dreams of ineffable depravity. Dreams of turmoils in which the sexuality was compulsive. Inability to distinguish reality from unreality.

Thus Mário became lost in a maze of presumed and concocted fantasies. Death then?

José Araújo seemed not to want to accept the evidence of an occurrence. Hôtel de Nice. 26 April.

The man lying on the bed with five phials of strychnine next to him. Assuming a prior event. This is what José Araújo suggested to me. Fear of sexuality, of paternal abandonment after his father had remarried or of poverty? Necessity to put an end to his life or only a fiction that ended poorly?, I asked.

Necessity!, replied José Araújo.

And then grumbling because he had reason to believe in a will extraneous to his own, that of Mário that is. A will that no longer belonged to him, José Araújo suggested a few moments later in a faint voice.

I understood the unnatural distinction that José Araújo was proposing to me.

Justifying a friend? Then madness seemed to score points in his favour. Schizophrenia. Therefore, nothing could be understood as will when it could well have been involuntary spontaneity.

José Araújo had the audacity to mention once again the name of Hélène, the prostitute who had subjugated Mário with her prostitute's charms.

Hélène the instigator of a suicide that was reasonably to be understood as a murder.

Hélène who had dragged Mário into a maelstrom from which it was difficult to escape. Charms, merely charms for a young man who had never experienced the sensual frenzy of physical love. A discovery that bothered someone, Mário that is, who had narrated sexual aberrations without ever having experienced them.

José Araújo seemed to want to reveal to me the most hidden aspect of the ambiguous sentiments that wounded Mário. Something, it seemed to me, of very great interest.

I had in some way elements suited for the investigative speculation of Dr Abílio Quaresma who was settled as best possible in Café Durant, at 2 Place de la Madeleine, where he was awaiting me.

Dr Abílio Quaresma would have attempted in every way to end our investigative adventure with a solution acceptable to Mr Craston, while he was certainly intent on downing a bottle of *Pastis* and while with the mind he wandered, for the umpteenth time, among the most complex and fascinating moves of the chess game between Akiba Rubinstein and Gersz Rotlewi.

XI

We sat facing each other without the desire to talk ... a glass of *pastis?*, I asked David Mondine to break an uneasy tension ... moments earlier, while we were standing next to the door of the Café Durant, I received accounts of his travels and of his suppositions concerning the completed investigations ... with a shake of his head he refused the invitation to have some *pastis*... he was exhausted, he told me ... especially for having violated a sad affair that did not seem to belong to a recognisable reality ... almost as if he had reviewed and re-examined it through a warped mirror ... then he mumbled that, in his opinion, it was an ambiguous affair marked by complex, unpleasant and deliberate deceits ... we then scrutinised each other in silence ... almost as if we were conversing with our eyes ... an ambiguous game, marked by irritating irreverence ... thus we imagined saying what should perhaps have been put into words ... and what would have been appropriate to be said in compliance with each other's temperament and intuitions ... we exchanged, in that oppressing silence, only comparisons and understandings that it was possible to exchange without pronouncing a word ... we realised, without any talk, that we were simply two individuals who had had the fate of chancing upon a rash investigation ... hence we would have to be reconciled, though without conviction, to come to a judgement that would appease the troubled mind of Fernando Pessoa ... in the silence, instead, we were falling into a dark maze of thoughts like a burden which corrodes minds ... we knew each other and we did not know each other in that silence ... it was difficult, in fact, to suppose, without speaking to each other, that there could exist in each of us another part of himself that could be combined with what was another ... therefore ambiguities and anxieties ... it was necessary to play the game that we had begun together ... restore roles, auspicious or inauspicious that they might be, because a story, indeed a certain story, drastically required a conclusion, whatever it might be ... meanwhile we were dealing with egocentric desires from which we were unable to escape ... in truth we then discovered, in scrutinising each other in that sort of initial silence, that we were not at all two strangers who distrusted each other, but that we were both called on to provide a solution to a dilemma that was already, in itself, solved in some way ... we had the task, it was clear to both of us, to provide an acceptable explanation of the causes of a death which were, in fact, evident ... we felt somehow obliged to define distinctive peculiarities and inappropriate and nefarious truths offending any honest thought ... we had to be, after all, ordinary and everyday subjects who responded to peculiar needs so as not to insult a memory, so as not to offend a man like Fernando Pessoa ... we had to imagine that they were indiscreet vices of the mind so that we could, with improbable boldness, take on bothersome and necessary roles ... we could also waste our time in hypotheses of very little truth and redeem ourselves with impudent and imprudent decisions to be taken ... the truth might not have been a single truth, I said to him loudly, sipping the *pastis*, and I continued affirming that, when it was not possible to establish that we were dealing with an absolute truth, we were faced with a *'principle'* of absolute truth ... for that dystonia we should, in fact, have been prepared to offer at least a plausible solution ... however, and it was necessary to clarify it, no one absolutely knew what *'principle of truth'* meant, since we did not know what was to be understood, in certain circumstances, as *'principle of truth'* ... neither of us could ever state that that was a principle of truth because, in reality, in each of us there was a singular truth in the moment in which there was imposed upon us, with an incoherent and senseless despotism, a certain and ambiguous truth ... hence we needed to discuss what we had to examine because Angus Craston and Fernando Pessoa desired that a matter be untangled, since this matter, to them, was an enigma when in fact it was only to be understood in all its ambiguous facets ... then I stopped talking and once again offered David Mondine a glass of *pastis* ... he accepted and sipped it with amiable tranquillity ... he looked at the bottom of the glass after the last drop ... he inhaled deeply, wiped the sweat from his brow and then murmured incomprehensible words, after which, with a pedantic tone, he asked me if I remembered who was Degenhard von Tegetthoff ... certain of my ignorance, he abruptly stated that it was Degenhard von Tegetthoff who defined, in a rather obscure but certainly very suggestive manner, the undefinable question of the duality of truth ... he looked at me for a few seconds and then added that Degenhard von Tegetthoff, as a Cartesian philosopher, had obtained in 1823 the chair of Ontological Gnosticism ... subsequently, in 1841 if I recall correctly, during a boat trip on the Titisee, he mysteriously disappeared ... his body was never found ... a voluntary departure and retreat to some remote hermitage was assumed because he was used to exploring, far away from men and things, his theory of '*Gewissensangst*[107]' ... in 1847 this supreme work of his appeared as a book ... in return, I asked if, in his opinion, unspecified disturbances molested minds predisposed to lacerating disquietudes ... in response David Mondine said that an unusual transience made it necessary to reason with oneself even amid tormenting paradoxes and incomprehensible qualms which had no other value if not to lead to an internal laceration ... to some that might have seemed an incipient madness, almost a delirium consumed in the attempt to recognise an interlocutor who, in reality, did not seem to exist ... fluctuating anguish and ambiguity ... we remained silent for a few moments ... I refilled the glasses and we downed the *pastis* at a good pace ... resuming the conversation I asked him if, in his opinion, one could speak of *pavor*, of a *pavor* so introjective as to determine the

107 Moral anxiety.

ineluctable necessity to transform soliloquies into real dialogues, as if they were something supremely redeeming ... thus if at first we were tempted to look with suspicion at that *pavor*, we slowly realised that the dialogue would have led us toward a truth which, although relative, would be able to convey the sensations of one's spirit to the other ... emotions and perceptions could thus become premises for a dialoguing disquisition in order to remove the *'pavor'* by playing, ambiguously, with a deliberate and integral conversational temerity ... David Mondine lingered on this point, recalling that, from readings of *Gewissensangst*, a volume in quarto published in Frankfurt am Main in 1847 by Weisenbach und Sohn, he had understood that an intricate nebula of verbal suggestions was able to heal any spirit predisposed to lacerations, what Degenhard von Tegetthoff called "*Teilung*[108]" .... moreover, Degenhard von Tegetthoff stated, recalled David Mondine, that a ruthless dualism, between self and other, as between self and reflected self, did not allow pacifications but only heated verbal disputes, while it was necessary to overcome the dualism and recognise oneself, also as a different part, in a *'unicum'*... after having drunk another two glasses of *pastis*, it seemed to me appropriate to reaffirm that I agreed with what he had told me because, in my opinion, by concealing a careless rationality one necessarily arrived at a servile and petulant dialogue with an alter ego, even as far as determining extravagant and disquieting dialectics ... to solve the investigative case that we had been assigned, we should, in my opinion, have given up some of our preconceived propositions ... in the end we should have done nothing else to pacify the souls of those who had been wounded by Mário Sá-Carneiro's ambiguous death than to understand if some morbid element had not found its way into Mário's mind so that he had taken to manifesting actions that did not depend on this or another mental element but only on the abstract use of reason ... David Mondine appeared pensive ... he poured another glass of *pastis* and instinctively

108 Guide.

replied that we had little time available to fully master intentions and language in proposing an acceptable account to Fernando Pessoa ... at the moment, in fact, we were not in possession of a plausible account since a sort of primitive anguish haunted us in the face of an absolutely incomprehensible death and the need to propose solutions acceptable to Fernando ... an ego and an alter ego?, I asked then ... David Mondine remained thoughtful for a few moments ... he repeatedly stole a glance at me... he sniffed the half-empty glass of *pastis* several times ... abruptly then he expressed his thoughts to me ... listening to him it was reasonable to wander with the mind among corrupt desires in order to provide reassuring news to Fernando ... therefore streets infested with diligent lies, with affirmations that deliberately contrasted with a reality that was not so, and we thus should have lingered in silent acquiescence, almost as if it were a hallucination to deceive those who wished to be deceived ... a feeble, dreamlike and hypocritical faith had to preside over our account to not demonstrate what there was to demonstrate ... barely a flash of banal consciousness had to preside over our revelations ... an imaginary understanding supported by deceptions almost as if they were intentions presided over by foul schemes which however should not have appeared as signs of a life consumed in a desolate, solitary, imaginary and mercenary deception ... what are we seeking deep down?, I asked David Mondine ... he did not reply immediately ... must we perpetuate a logorrhoeic delirium of falsehood?, I added questioningly ... David Mondine reflected, once again filling his glass with *pastis* ... he shook his head ... he made a gesture of a toast, raising his glass on high ... then he downed the liquor in a single gulp and began to ramble on ... an effect of alcohol?, I don't know ... certainly he came out with words that seemed to me senseless ... he philosophised with ambiguous acumen, maintaining that it was reasonable to be inspired by what is contained in books dealing with deception and ambiguity, even though they contained worn-out ideas wounded by time, albeit registered as redeeming memory ... I thought it wise then to ask if his desire referred to a simple sensation, because it seemed to me unjust to report it as a possible conclusion of our investigation, almost as if it were a kind of imprudent and impudent solution, something which I did not wish to share because, I explained, I am in possession only of common senses without documented justifications able to accept subterfuges or deceptions ... then there was a prolonged silence ... David Mondine looked at me with scepticism ... he sighed and replied polemically that it was necessary to provide information or a communication intratextual between saying and not saying, between affirming and denying ... in short, it was necessary to refer to an ambiguous awareness of the causes of Mário's death and this was possible because each of us preserved, in some corner of his conscience, an indefinable and obscure compromise ... also an infinite desolation of lying, if necessary ... in certain circumstances it was necessary to pretend not to want and not to be able to discern what might be appropriate to discern ... in other words, deceive, with scrupulous but elusive words, our Fernando ... I had other thoughts and I did not hesitate to reveal them to him, so I whispered that, in my opinion, it was absolutely impossible to provide Fernando Pessoa with an investigative conclusion without a preliminary, detailed and careful analysis, instead of taking recourse to a hasty examination or to what people unable to think call intuition, even if it was more practical to proceed in this way ... he seemed to be troubled by my words ... he looked away and, staring at the now empty glass of *pastis*, replied that his behaviour should not be considered perverse ... nothing else, in fact, was possible if not the opportunity to propose what might have been a possible and occurred eventuality ... in those circumstances it was necessary and appropriate, so as not to hurt other people's feelings, to yield to ambiguity and propose a reassuring message, albeit practising a spurious truth ... an enunciation anything but irresponsible since it was desired to grant to those who had given us an assignment, in particular Fernando, a salutary safeguard of his conscience ... it was also necessary to propose an improper solution since, on 31 March, Mário had written to Fernando that he had lived his last happy day ... that he was very content ... that a thousand years separated him from tomorrow ... that he marvelled only at the tranquillity of things because he saw them more clearly, with sharper outlines because soon he would have to abandon them ... was it a sign of madness in the determination that ... a decision already taken then? ... and yet this did not convince me because I've always thought that in any investigation of an incident whose nature was unknown it was important to isolate any unexpected and strange element ... Mário's death presented several incongruities ... could it be considered a death as a medicinal panacea in the face of uncontrollable desires, but also a demonstrative act? ... also an attempt to involve others in a weary melancholy that no one could understand? ... I posed these questions to David Mondine with a critical tone ... he did not hesitate for a moment ... he replied right away, exclaiming that it could obviously have been a medicinal panacea ... or rather a certain rash ethics ... a sort of ethics born from the mind of a foolish pretender: using a lexicon so dear to Fernando Pessoa ... and he continued after downing another glass of *pastis* ... his voice was slightly impaired by the alcohol, he had trouble talking when he added that Mário was certainly a pretender without realising it and that he had realised that he was able to manoeuvre with a twofold or threefold or fourfold possibility of exterior lives according to need ... he could have consciously practised a rash usury regarding the feelings of others ... could it be?, I then asked him abruptly, filling his glass once again ... Mondine's unsuitable inebriation favoured my critical spirit ... he did not respond immediately ... he seemed to be meditating ... he sipped the *pastis* slowly ... he narrowed his eyes for an instant ... then certainly heartened by thoughts that must have seemed to him adequate for a plausible response he muttered that it was necessary to consider every event in Mário's life starting with the fact that he had been deprived of comforting maternal affection and had not been able to exercise a sort of ethical self-control, allowing himself to be overcome by a vulgar moralism, the inquisitor of himself ... I replied with some passion, declaring that his speech was no more than a kind of sermon reiterated like an adulatory panegyric to Mário who had become annoyingly petulant with the passing of the years, no longer able to avoid justificatory thoughts ... Mário's convictions were corroded by immoral speculations when it came to judging the loss of affection from a father lost in the abyss of narcissism ... I added further that, in my opinion, Mário should have sought at least an emotional compromise that he had always avoided for ... yes: for what? ... perhaps for the unconditional and total acceptance of bizarre behaviours? ... after his mother died, there was nothing else for Mário but to refer to himself ... almost as if the mother's loss was a widowhood irreconcilable with all sane mental thoughts ... thus he had gone well beyond any normal certainty and had sunk into a paradoxical sense of solitude ... an unjust outrage?, perhaps ... yet looking well at it, it was for Mário the only possibility left to him to give meaning to what might have been called ethics ... a second-rate ethics ... it seemed to me, I added, almost as if he wanted to trade his sanity for perverse madness ... thus I asked David Mondine if he thought that there was an ethical norm that prohibited trading one's sanity ... I asked the question with a rhetorical tone and I suggested that mine was merely an ambiguous and superficial distinction between good and evil ... or perhaps just a linguistic compromise so that we could justify a certain attitude of Mário ... it was sufficient to recall the ambiguous letter that Mário's father had written to his father, Mário's grandfather, on 5 August 1904 in which he stated that Mário was well ... he had no malaise ... he was beginning to get on by himself ... was he really well? ... thus choosing hypocrisy and allowing Mário to definitively sink into the fog of disaffection ... at least that's how it seemed to me ... David Mondine, now drunk from *pastis* and with muddled words, replied that perhaps Mário wished to go well beyond any spectral city of the mind ... to think poorly of other people's negligences and lies ... in short, become lost amidst the shadows of irrationality ... a turning point in his life could have come only from full and satisfactory sexuality, which unfortunately Mário did not know ... hence there remained nothing else but to appease himself with the absurdity of a desired madness since Mário went about in solitude constantly becoming lost amidst the bizarre tangles of the mind ... at times he thought that he could even confess to himself ... no heteronyms, just another himself ... the one facing the other ... one in front of the other ... one behind the other ... a duplicating, obsessive reiteration ... nothing that could ever have been different ... not even the mirrors could define the true entities ... he lacked a space for survival ... he was navigating alone in a warped memory ... David Mondine abruptly fell silent ... only for a few moments and then he resumed pouring forth words exactly when I wished to intervene ... the alcohol had become a sovereign spur to his chattering ... sense and nonsense ... confused dialogue ... a rapid back and forth ... ambiguous phrases ... one of us then said: – remember what happened ... the other replied: – what? ... and it continued without pause or respect for the other's words ... no prejudices, he murmured ... what? ... insight into one's ambiguous existence ... does it mean awareness? ... a hypothetical value that has foundation exactly in its ambiguity ... irreplaceable since indefinable? ... ambiguous tangibility as a hesitant murder or suicide if you wish ... then perhaps he could have had insight into his existence? ... these seemed to me to be petty subtleties ... fruitlessness of a mental crisis ... fruitlessness of his conscience? ... a hesitant murder remained valid and whoever had committed that murder certainly had a name ... was it sufficient to look around? ... difficult in a concatenated succession of events ... and the past? ... hesitant murder ... being able to alter reality ... and the intimations of memory? ... limitations ... in essence was it necessary to believe only in a hesitant murder? ... there had happened what had to happen ... to observe a ritual? ... an extreme and inevitable moment ... resuming life in the moment in which he had inopportunely left it? ... perhaps it would have been sufficient to assume that it had a value ... life–death ... a warped dichotomy? ... everything began with the void left by the death of a mother ... then someone killed himself at ten in the morning in a courtyard of a school in front of his teachers and classmates ... it was impossible to forget ... Tomás Cabreira Júnior, in fact ... an unfortunate incident which became for Mário a stigma of a time ... feeding then on illusions? ... schizophrenic ornament of a fictional reality ... desperately cultivating images lost in a crystallised memory ... narcissist violence? ... a subtle and perverse game ... it all began on that 9 January 1911, at ten in the morning ... did Mário then try to hide the truth from his moribund self? ... another hesitant murder ... an act intended as an affirmation of his personality ... a victory born from a failure? ... someone looked at Tomás with admiration and bewilderment ... it remained only to be reflected in terrifying mirrors that intertwined his images ... then Mário understood what death meant ... David and I fell silent exhausted ... we looked at each other ... foreheads moist with sweat ... it was necessary then to refill our glasses and quickly down the *pastis* ... we took to glancing around ... a morass of uninteresting faces ... perhaps we wished for nothing more ... hard to find a solution to offer to Fernando Pessoa ... then we toasted with another glass of *pastis*, repeatedly squinting, conquered by the torpor of a tedious inebriation ... then we began to pour forth senseless discourses in an unnatural mumbling due to our libations ... we even finished talking about death ... an obsession that seemed the only viable path ... like solitude, for that matter ... and that seemed able to satisfy us ... evading a reality that was distressing ... seeking refuge in fantastic, non-existent, imagined thoughts ... in places of the mind ... then it would be possible to versify with Orpheus's song ... a disgusting song of love ... and then justly lamenting beyond any whim ... it would have been sufficient to throw kisses to the mirror ... an unfortunate destiny would have been accomplished ... we were strangers to ourselves ... thus living a life consisting of days that were always the same ... obsessively boring ... inadequately petulant ... here then, as reported by some acquaintances, a flabby body that sought to conceal vices and virtues ... why had Mário not returned to Lisbon and had not taken his place at a table of the café A Brasileira so that some father could see him? ... maybe it was impossible that a father would have noticed him ... only travels and other loves ... meanwhile a son was mollified by the affections of servants ... no longer a participant in reality ... what to say? ... just apathy, malaise and tedium ... thus pretending to be the dirty reflection of an image ... what to feel then? ... bewilderment, only bewilderment ... what could he have felt? ... being suborned to a will that did not belong, dealing with the ominous task of living ... finding himself to be a monster of unhappy wisdom ... created perhaps to satisfy a baleful rituality ... remembrances of what had been and the foresight of what should have been ... losing himself in regrets and the solitudes of soliloquies ... also immobile because embalmed in a thick layer of fat that hindered his movements ... thus Mário would have seen horrible incidents as a prophesying lackey ... just an image and not being anything else ... perhaps he should have remembered *Amizade*[109] ... paying homage to or exorcising death ... the spectacle was always a spectacle ... a naive intention to deceive himself ... a stage should have changed sentiments ... how many sacrifices just to recite in life ... to conceal from himself every unhealthy mood ... an ominous mood had become a judge of a lost state of mind ... *Amizade*? ... death-spectacle ... considering reasonable the spirit devoted to pain ... unfulfilled, restless spirit ... many the reasons and many the disappointments ... thus offering false ambiguities ... acting with senseless polemic ... and comparing who was the actor with who participated in the recital of life ... accommodating, conciliatory, meek actors ... leaving themselves to be corrupted by aggressive spectators ... falsehood was not only what was being shown on a dilapidated stage ... a mirror of a troubled life ... a never-resolved dispute ... a game of sides ... also an incoherent dispute ... we were who we were, without managing to understand the reality of the dispute ... life as theatre and theatre as life ... contests between those who lived to act and those who acted to live ... *Amizade*, in fact ... a debt to pay ...

---

109 Play in three acts by Mário de Sá-Carneiro. First performed on 23 March 1912.

Tomás Cabreira Júnior had been co-author ... what else to say except to have wished to speak with those who offered themselves spontaneously ... to foment disputes? ... to live or die in order to know if it was appropriate to live or die ... playing on basic misunderstandings ... competing in a dispute ... impulsive melodrama ... ambiguous desires given in to hidden interests ... also reflections of a state of mind ... the stage as an ontological contradiction ... 23 March 1912, *Amizade* ... a scenic game to revive the sense of theatricality of life ... a trivial polemic to obtain an ambiguous conclusion ... not certifying any truth ... finding a buffer against anguish ... also a buffer against nefarious solitude ... amusing oneself practising ambiguity ... thus bridling any indefinable value ... reasoning about each heart-rending or allaying incident ... a life of the stage and a stage of life ... a dream as remarkable glory ... abandoning the scene of life without hesitation ... facing existence even though complaining about it ... a funeral could suddenly appear from an angle ... also a resounding death, masked by joyous theatrical ceremony ... *Amizade,* then ... it was only a hymn to a troubled awareness of an ancient affection ... even without a father lost as he was in petty adventures of life outside the stage of life ... even without a woman who yielded herself ... wanting then to be a woman ... sex as a human relationship ... bowing to enigmatic aberrations ... ambiguous questions ... playing with established habits and troubled irrationality ... illogical considerations ... saving himself with a compromise ... extricating himself from an unjust alienation ... debased humanity... having sex to overcome congenital inhibitions? ... also a prevailing solitude ... sheltering behind the most horrid aberrations ... no longer being able to think of another human being ... amassed faces ... mouths open ... twisted limbs ... renouncing any living space ... voices ... claiming to be a *'human'* while knowing that he was not ... derelicts exhausted by loneliness ... dying before being born ... suicide of a species ... taxonomy of the lowest level ... human species ... slowly dying ... exalting sex as a last hope ... warding off solitude or practising a spectacle-suicide? ... my rambling expression of thoughts abruptly ceased ... David Mondine lay sleeping with his head resting in his folded arms ... I sucked the last drops of *pastis* from the bottle... then I pulled from a pocket my chess set and placed the pieces as they were positioned before the last move Akiba Rubinstein made against Gersz Rotlewi ... immobile I admired the brilliance of that action ... just before that move Gersz Rotlewi had committed suicide in some way with his last move ... a conscious or unconscious act? ... like Mário, after all, Gersz Rotlewi had failed to control his instinctual concerns ... like Mário, was that of Gersz Rotlewi a foolish hesitant murder or perhaps a conscious, foolhardy suicide? ... it was more than legitimate, therefore, to offer to Fernando Pessoa this disjunctive proposition as the result of the investigation of Mário Sá-Carneiro's death ... and so it was!

Lightning Source UK Ltd.
Milton Keynes UK
UKOW04f0610290817
308156UK00001B/306/P